SMALL-TOWN DREAMS

SMALL-TOWN DREAMS

Julie Ellis

Severn House Large Print
London & New York

This first large print edition published in Great Britain 2005 by
SEVERN HOUSE LARGE PRINT BOOKS LTD of
9-15 High Street, Sutton, Surrey, SM1 1DF.
First world regular print edition published 2004 by
Severn House Publishers, London and New York.
This first large print edition published in the USA 2005 by
SEVERN HOUSE PUBLISHERS INC., of
595 Madison Avenue, New York, NY 10022.

British Library Cataloguing in Publication Data

Ellis, Julie, 1933 -
    Small town dreams - Large print ed.
    1.   Women teachers - New York (State) - Fiction
    2.   Women veterans - New York (State) - Fiction
    3.   United States - Social life and customs - 1945-1970 - Fiction
    4.   New York (State) - Fiction
    5.   Large type books
    I.   Title
    813.5'4 [F]

ISBN 0-7278-7425-X

Printed and bound in Great Britain by
MPG Books Ltd, Bodmin, Cornwall.

To Vanessa Holt and Philip

One

Laurie Evans sat on a corner of the living room sofa in her brother and sister-in-law's apartment in Manhattan's West 80s. Long slim legs tucked beneath her, one hand sweeping through her short, dark hair. Three large valises and sundry cartons containing her books, newly acquired television set, and sundry collectibles were stacked against one wall. Her own apartment released to her landlord, happy with this in the current rental climate. Her rebellious blue eyes were in sharp contrast to the indulgent smile she contrived as Tim scolded her.

'You did the smart thing to go back to college after the war, to earn your BA and masters in education,' he conceded. 'Then all of a sudden three months ago – before you even had your teaching license – you decide you don't want to teach in New York.' His voice exuded exasperation. 'Where the hell did you get the weird idea that small towns are perfect?'

'I didn't say they were,' Laurie hedged.

'But this is 1950 – the war's been over for five years. I just want to live a quiet, normal life.'

'You can do that without moving to the ends of the world,' Tim said grimly.

'Bentonville isn't the end of the world – it's three hours from here. It's a beautiful little town—'

'You're out of your mind!' Tim shook his head in disbelief. 'How can you isolate yourself in the boondocks after the kind of life you've always lived?'

'Because of the kind of life I've lived.' Okay, that was part of it. How could she explain to Tim and Iris the demons that battled within her? This wasn't a sudden decision – she'd been working up to it for the past six years. 'Tim, we've both spent most of our lives chasing around from one part of the world to another.' *Other kids who knew us thought, 'Wow, how exciting to live in Paris and Rome and Istanbul and Hong Kong!'* 'I spent seventeen months in Italy with the WACs. Now I want roots.'

'You can have roots right here,' Tim shot back.

'What about an apartment somewhere in Westchester?' Iris intervened. 'Maybe in Dobbs Ferry.' One of the few Westchester towns that offered apartments. 'That's small-town living without giving up city advantages. Tim and I have it both ways when we close next month on the house in Ardsley.'

'You'll be sleeping in Ardsley,' Laurie scoffed. 'You'll be chasing back and forth on the highway five or six days a week. I don't want suburbia. I want to live twenty-four hours a day, seven days a week in a small town where people aren't too busy to say "good-morning", where everybody knows everybody else.'

'And everybody knows everybody else's business,' Tim jeered.

'In small towns people care about one another. They're there to help when emergencies arise—'

'Laurie, you've been watching too many movies.' Tim shook his head in frustration.

'You and Iris have lived here three years. How many people do you know in this building?' Laurie challenged.

Tim ignored this. 'A small town is no place for a single girl—'

'You'll never meet an interesting man there,' Iris added.

'I don't *want* to meet an interesting man. I don't want to get married. I like being single.'

'But people in Bentonville won't know that,' Iris pounced. 'You'll be a stranger in town – out to snare one of their young men. You'll be a pariah.'

'Their eligible young men will be safe.

They'll get the message fast enough.' Defiance crept into her voice. *They don't believe me, do they? About meaning to stay single.*

'In small towns single girls live at home,' Tim pointed out. 'With their families.' Their father and mother had died in a plane crash when she was sixteen and Tim twenty-one. 'And why in hell did you break up with Phil?' So far they'd accepted her explanations that 'it just wasn't working out for us'. 'He's a great guy. A war hero.' *So Phil spent three years fighting in the South Pacific. I was right behind the Fifth Army in Italy. And I wasn't baking cookies.*

'I was out of my mind to get involved with Phil. I wasn't in love with him. I had this crazy idea that with him I might have roots. I—'

'You would have,' Tim shot back.

'The wrong roots,' Laurie rejected. 'I'd hate the kind of life Phil wants. Thank God, I had the sense to break up with him.'

Her mind darted back eleven weeks – to the evening she'd had dinner with Phil at a restaurant he'd discovered in lower Westchester.

'You'll love it,' he promised as they headed up the West Side Highway. 'It sits beside a pond, with a pair of elegant swans in residence. Très romantic.'

Dinner was superb – and expensive. But

Phil was celebrating his graduation from law school and the well-paying job waiting for him in the law firm headed by his father.

'Hey, isn't it about time we announced our engagement?' he prodded over a sumptuous dessert. They'd been going steady for a year – both graduate students at Columbia. 'My folks are already hinting they'll help with the down-payment on a house. Somewhere up here.' He reached across the table for her hand. 'Maybe near Tim and Iris.'

'Let's settle into our jobs before we think about where we'll live.' They'd been too busy with school and part-time jobs to look that far ahead. *He's talking about a house in suburbia. Ugh!*

'You've said a hundred times how you're sick of being awakened at five a.m. by garbage trucks. How you hate the subway madness, and the traffic noises. You—'

'You have to take the bar exams,' she interrupted. 'I have to apply for my teaching license, land a job. Of course, if I find something for the coming school year it'll be a small miracle. But I can substitute—'

'Honey, you don't have to worry about teaching.' He chuckled indulgently. 'I'll be able to support us.'

She stared at him in shock. *What does he mean?* 'I want to teach.' *Why else did I go for my master's in education?*

11

'How long would you teach, anyway? We both want kids—'

'Why should that prevent me from teaching?' Warning signals jiggled in her brain. 'All right, I'll have to take maternity leave for a while.'

'Why would you want to teach? You'll be running the house, raising the kids.' His smile was fatuous. *This is a stranger sitting across the table from me.* 'Mom said she'll show you how to make all my favorite dishes. We'll have to entertain clients – it's part of the business. Mom will clue you in on how to handle small dinner parties. We'll—'

'No,' Laurie broke in, her heart pounding in rejection. 'I'm going to teach. And I'd detest living in suburbia.' She shuddered at the prospect.

'A house of our own on a nice-sized plot. Not some dreary apartment in the city. That's the Great American Dream.'

'I saw *Mr Blanding Builds His Dream House*. Suburbia isn't my Great American Dream.'

'You're always talking about yearning for roots,' he reiterated. 'That means a house and family.' His eyes were accusing. 'We'll get a GI mortgage—'

'You're moving too fast,' she reproached, fighting panic.

'I spent three years fighting a war.' He was

grim in recall. 'After that two more years in college, then three years in law school. I—'

'I went back to school, too,' she reminded. Thanks to the GI Bill their generation would be the best-educated in history. 'Am I supposed to throw away all that education?'

'It's time to settle down. Have a life.'

'We can have a life in Manhattan.' *He's staring at me as though I have two heads.* 'I have every intention of teaching – even with a family. Women do that now.'

'Not my wife.' The atmosphere was supercharged. *We're like two gladiators in an arena.* 'My wife will stay home – where she belongs.'

'Not me,' she defied. 'I won't go back to the way things were before the war. Women went out into the world, saw a whole different life. You can't shove us back into the closet and slam the door closed.' She thought about Eve – her best friend all through the college and grad school years – who was down in Georgia now combining teaching with volunteer work with the NAACP. Lois – her apartment-mate during grad school – who'd gone from a degree in journalism to working on a Manhattan newspaper and since July had been a foreign correspondent in Korea. During the war years Lois ferried planes for Jacqueline Cochran. 'We've seen that other world, and

13

we like it.'

'You're out of your mind!' he yelled. 'The war was an emergency – it wasn't natural. This is what comes of your being a WAC! Women had no right being in the armed forces. You should have stayed home – where you belonged.'

Laurie seethed with rage. 'I won't go back. A lot of us won't.' Her mind darted back to the war years. There were men who had welcomed WACs beside them, had seen women in service as part of the team first and women second. And there'd been others – like Phil. 'Find yourself another girl, Phil. One who's satisfied to be a second-class citizen.'

'Laurie, you're leaving us.' Iris brought her back to the moment. 'Come back.'

'I'm sorry. I was thinking about the break-up with Phil. It finally got through to me that we have different visions of the future. He didn't want me to teach after we were married. He wanted me home baking cookies and waxing floors and taking care of the kids.'

Iris sighed. 'A lot of guys came back from fighting with that vision of the future. And a lot of women are happy to go along with that.'

'Not this woman!'

'But most women are. Look at the way

marriage statistics have jumped up in the last four years – and the birth rate. But some of us,' Iris turned to Tim with a teasing smile, 'like Laurie said, don't want to go back to life the way it was before the war.' Iris had been a 'government girl' down in Washington for almost three wartime years. That was where she'd met Tim – when he'd been between foreign correspondent assignments.

'You know, Iris, I don't expect you to give up your job until you want to.' Tim was defensive. Iris loved her job in TV – and she was moving ahead career-wise.

'Phil doesn't feel the way you do, Tim. He thinks a working wife is a threat to his manhood.' Laurie's tone was scathing. She and Phil had been so busy with school until May and graduation that they hadn't talked much about the future. Getting their degrees was what was important. 'Thank God, I found out in time. I don't have to be married to put down roots.'

'It helps—' Tim was reproachful.

'I'll love teaching – in a small town. Suburbia is a hybrid. In Bentonville I'll meet people, join groups, become involved in the community. I'll have my work. Bentonville isn't at the end of the world.'

Fate had taken a hand, she thought gratefully. A miracle that she found a teaching job at the last moment. In a town she picked at random.

'I'll come down here to visit you two on holidays – or you'll come up to Bentonville to visit with me.' *I don't need a man in my life to have roots.*

She and Tim had always been very close – probably because of their peripatetic lives until college years. And there was that other angle. Her mind insisted on honesty. Mom and Dad had loved them, did everything that was right for them. Yet there was something in their love that didn't quite allow anyone else – even their son and daughter – inside their magic inner circle of two. That had built the closeness between Tim and her.

'Look, if you realize it's been a ghastly mistake, you can always come and stay with us until you get your act together.' Iris exchanged a confirming glance with Tim.

'With the baby boom what it is,' Tim said, chuckling, 'there'll always be teaching jobs available in New York.'

'I'll remember,' Laurie promised.

But she meant to settle down in Bentonville, New York. Not in Manhattan. Not in suburbia. In small-town USA – where neighbors cared about one another.

She'd rented a furnished apartment in a private house – from such a nice, reserved semi-retired couple. Mrs Kendrick was letting the telephone man into the apartment to install her phone. She'd explained that her husband did handyman jobs around town.

'So if you need any help at all, just tell us and Bud will be right over.'

She had an open-end lease so that when the right time arrived she could move out into a little house of her own. Property was much less expensive up in Bentonville than it was in Manhattan or Westchester County – where Tim and Iris were buying. They considered themselves lucky to find a house in Ardsley for sixteen thousand.

She still had a small chunk of her inheritance from their parents – even after buying the car. That would be a down-payment on an inexpensive little house, where the GI mortgage payments would be low. And under the GI Bill she could get a mortgage. Tim said no bank in the country would give a single woman a mortgage – except under the GI Bill.

'We'd better hit the sack soon.' Tim cleared his throat in a way that betrayed his unease at her putting such distance between them. During the war years putting much distance between them had been unavoidable, of course. 'We'll be getting up early to see you off.' Tomorrow was the Friday before the Labor Day weekend. Laurie wanted to be on the road early – before the traffic became insane. 'But first, let's watch the late news. See what's happening in Korea.'

On June 25th Communist North Korea had invaded South Korea – intensifying American anxiety about Communist aggression. With the backing of the UN President Truman ordered American GIs to the defense of South Korea.

Laurie and Iris settled on the sofa while Tim fiddled with the dials of their recently acquired television set with a twelve-inch screen. He'd been prompted to buy – after months of ridiculing the industry for the quality of its programs – by the beginning of the Korean conflict. Nobody called it a war – it was a 'police action' according to Washington and the UN. But American soldiers were dying there.

'Thank God, Tim has had his fill of war,' Iris said with a bright smile, but Laurie knew her sister-in-law harbored fears that Tim would want to go to cover the Korean 'police action' if it continued much longer.

'We've both had our share,' Laurie said softly, hoping to reassure Iris. She'd been only thirteen years old when Tim took off to fight with the Abraham Lincoln Brigade in Spain, but she still remembered her terror at the dangers that he was facing.

'Okay, shut up and let's see what's the latest,' Tim ordered.

'Ever since we bought the TV set last

month, you have to watch every news program,' Iris joshed. 'Next thing I know, you'll
be deserting the magazine to go chasing
over to Korea. And I'll be stuck with the
house in Ardsley.'

'No way.' Tim grinned – content to ignore
the commercial. 'Those eleven months in
Spain plus almost four years as a war
correspondent made me appreciate being in
one place.' The eardrum punctured in Spain
had kept him from fighting in World War II.
'I'm staying at my desk at the magazine
until they put me out to pasture.'

'You remember that,' Iris said with mock
sternness. 'I don't want a husband who's
chasing all over the globe.' She turned to
Laurie – her face tender. 'I guess – like you
– I want roots. Wherever that might be.'

'There you go,' Tim jibed. 'You women
always stick together.'

Two

Tonight Laurie found sleep elusive. Why had she allowed herself to become involved that way with Phil? In a corner of her mind she'd told herself it was the normal thing to do. Her own small circle of friends were either married or thinking about it.

She'd conned herself into believing she and Phil had a lot in common, but they hardly knew each other. They were both working so hard for their degrees, holding down part-time jobs at the same time. They'd met at a book store across from Columbia. They spent what little free time they had together. Catching a movie, going to a museum, walking along the river discussing politics – but not often in agreement. When they could take time to read, he devoured Zane Grey. She read Faulkner. At intervals they'd indulged in heavy petting – because it was 'what everybody did'. She never allowed them to go 'all the way'. Phil hadn't been happy about that.

'Honey, look at the statistics,' he'd argue. That meant the Kinsey Report. 'Two out of three single women have premarital sex.'

'Then the report says fifty per cent don't,' she pointed out. 'The math's screwed up.'

He'd sulk briefly, then get over it. But at regular intervals she wondered if she was frigid. She considered this for a moment. Had she enjoyed the physical side of their relationship? Yes – but she could survive without it, she told herself. No big deal.

Back in high school – the family now New York City residents – she had talked a lot about that with Peg and Janie. She remembered the afternoon Janie had called her with much excitement...

'Laurie, come over to our apartment tonight.' Janie and her family lived right across the street. 'Peg's coming, too. My folks are going to the theater.' Janie's father was a doctor, and Janie – at fourteen – was sure he must have books that talked about *that*. 'They won't be home until close to midnight.'

'I'll come over right after dinner,' Laurie promised, her eyes bright with anticipation.

'I'll say you and Peg are coming over to study with me for a test,' Janie improvised.

Laurie and Peg arrived almost at the same moment – just as Janie's parents were leaving. They watched from a front window while Mr and Mrs Lawson climbed into a taxi.

21

'They've gone.' Still, Janie lowered her voice. 'I found a book in Daddy's office. Not just a medical book – a manual,' she announced in triumph. 'I'll go get it.' Janie hurried from the living room, returned moments later. 'Okay,' she said, faintly breathless. 'Let's read.'

The three girls sat on the plush beige carpeting and page by page explored the manual. So this was not the medical text that Janie had expected to find in her father's small home office. *This was better.*

'Wow!' Peg leaned back against the sofa. 'Can you imagine your parents doing that?' She shivered expressively.

'I guess when you're grown up it's okay,' Janie decided.

'Yeah,' Laurie agreed. 'When you're married.'

Laurie brushed aside the recall. She'd never get to sleep digging into the past this way. But her mind dwelled for a few moments on those high school years, when she and Peg and Janie had adored Tyrone Power and Clark Gable.

Finally she drifted off into restless slumber. She awoke almost an hour before her alarm clock was set to go off. She lay back against the pillows on her improvised bed on the living room sofa and geared herself for the momentous day that lay ahead. The first day of the rest of her life. Tim was anxious for her – but she was realizing a dream.

Seven floors below a sanitation truck was making a raucous pick-up. In the same vicinity an impatient driver leaned on a horn. She was leaving behind the ugly noises that made up city life. Tomorrow morning she'd wake up to the beautiful sound of birds singing in the trees outside her bedroom window. No more battles with crowded subway cars – she'd walk to her destination or drive.

Moving quietly about the apartment so as not to disturb Tim or Iris any earlier than necessary, she prepared for the day ahead. Showered, dressed in her favorite dungarees, a white cotton shirt and matching flat-heeled shoes, she applied make-up, then focused on returning the living room to its normal appearance.

Now she was conscious of a soaring excitement. A dream was about to become reality. Today she was driving up to Bentonville to stay.

Her mind darted back through the years to her last momentous move. January 1944 and she was leaving the Manhattan apartment for her basic training center. She was under age – enrollment required that prospective WACs be twenty years old. But because Tim – as her legal guardian since their parents died two years earlier – signed for her, she was allowed to join at eighteen.

She suspected that Tim was relieved when she had insisted on joining the WACs. He worried about her when he dashed off on foreign correspondent assignments. He felt she was safe in service. And in an odd way they both felt as though she was serving in his stead.

A reminiscent smile lit her face. Neither of them anticipated that she would be jumping into dugouts, dodging bombs along with male GIs in the arduous battle for Italy. Neither of them envisioned her wearing enlisted men's pants, shirts, and combat boots in those months of trudging up Italian mountains. Living in tents in the dead of winter. Nor had either of them anticipated the contemptuous reaction of many Americans towards the women who joined the WACs. Even some GIs resented their presence in the armed forces – and made this clear. But enough of this, she chided herself. Look ahead, not backward.

She knew the route upstate – she'd made the trip three times now. Once she went to check out the town. The next time was for her job interview. Then she had to drive up to rent an apartment – of which there were few in Bentonville. It was a relief when she located a vacancy.

In a flurry of nervousness she reached for

her purse, looked to make sure the apartment key was there. She remembered the Kendricks were leaving this morning for a long Labor Day weekend in Montreal, where they had family. The telephone was supposed to be installed yesterday – the service man to be admitted by Mrs Kendrick. It had been taken care of, hadn't it? She'd feel stranded without a phone.

Also earlier than planned, Tim and Iris arose for the day.

'It's going to be hot as hell,' Iris warned. 'Is there a fan up in your apartment in Bentonville?'

'I didn't notice.' But Laurie wasn't concerned. 'Anyhow, it's probably ten degrees cooler up there.'

'People sweat in Bentonville, too,' Tim warned. 'And this weekend's supposed to be a scorcher.' Already the apartment was uncomfortably humid despite the living room window fan.

Iris made breakfast with determined high spirits. Laurie reflected her mood. *Why must Tim persist in seeming so scared for me? I'm twenty-four years old. Almost twenty-five. I've spent seventeen months in army uniform in a war zone. What bad can happen to me in a serene, lovely town of 8,000?*

At a few minutes before 9 a.m. – the trunk and rear seat of her new Dodge crammed to capacity, her good-byes said – she headed for the West Side Highway. Not a minute too early, she told herself. The holiday traffic was already in evidence.

On Tuesday morning she was to report to the school. On Wednesday morning classes would begin. Of course, she'd be nervous the first few days of teaching. This wasn't student teaching. But she loved kids – and third graders wouldn't be too demanding. Classes would be small – the Bentonville Board of Ed prided itself on that. The staff – the school included kindergarten through twelfth grade – would be friendly. Everybody in small towns was friendly, she thought with recurrent pleasure.

Impatient when traffic slowed to a standstill, she reached to flip on the car radio. She heard the tail end of the Korean news. The Allies were optimistic despite outraged reports that the Reds were killing prisoners. There was talk among General MacArthur's spokesmen of a possible victory by Thanksgiving.

The news from Korea was followed by the latest on Senator Joe McCarthy's tirades about Communists in the government. Back in February he claimed that he had the names of 205 card-carrying Communists working in the State Department. Sure, the country was furious at Communists – both in the USSR, in North Korea, and here at home – but weren't people like McCarthy whipping up hysteria in this country?

Laurie recalled what she'd read of the Senate report on McCarthy's accusations: 'At a time when American blood is again being shed to preserve our dream of freedom, we are constrained fearlessly and frankly to call the charges what they truly are: a fraud and a hoax.'

Everybody knew, Laurie thought with contempt, that Senator McCarthy was out to destroy President Truman and Dean Acheson.

Still, she was conscious of some trepidation when – after almost six hours of bumper-to-bumper traffic – she drove into Bentonville. The air of serenity that the town radiated was like a warm, loving embrace. She drove down the three-block stretch that was the business section with a sense of coming home. No building rose above four stories – most no more than one. The wide Main Street was divided by a narrow island that offered a display of greenery and late-summer flowers. People walked about the streets at a casual pace – none of the air of frenzy that was part of big-city life.

The Kendrick house – a five-minute walk to town – was a white miniature Victorian set on a 75 x 100 foot plot. The Kendricks had divided off a one-bedroom apartment with its own side entrance as a rental.

All the houses in the area appeared to have been built years earlier but were maintained with pride. Well-trimmed shrubbery, late summer flowers in colorful display. She swung into the Kendricks' driveway with a sense of belonging. She left the car, walked up the narrow flagstone path that led to the entrance to her apartment. She was home – part of this town now.

She slid the key into place, frowned. *Why isn't it turning? What's wrong?* She stared, perplexed. Yes, this was the key Mrs Kendrick had given her. Try again, she ordered herself. But it was futile.

Mrs Kendrick must have given me the wrong key. And they won't be back until Tuesday morning!

She glanced speculatively about the house. She wasn't about to take up residence in the car. Okay, try to open a window. The first one was locked. The second inched upward a bit, then balked.

There's a screwdriver in the glove compartment of the car. Try that.

Three

In the modest, Tudor-inspired house directly opposite the Kendricks' residence Beth Winston – a slender, trim woman in her mid-fifties – abruptly stopped watering the red geraniums in one of the window boxes.

Her eyes fastened to the house across the way, she called to her son. 'Neil! Somebody's trying to break into the Kendricks' house!'

'In broad daylight?' he scoffed. But he abandoned the book he was reading to join her. He glanced out the window. Whistled softly. 'That's nerve.'

'Neil, be careful,' Mrs Winston warned. He was already charging towards the front door.

Out of the house, he hurried across the street, approached the small, slender, very pretty girl working with a screwdriver at a window. 'People around here prefer to use a door key.'

She glanced up, exasperated. 'It won't work.'

'The Kendricks are away for the weekend.

Though you probably know that.' His eyes were reproachful. For some absurd reason he hoped she'd have a satisfactory explanation.

'Of course I know that,' she shot back. Comprehension broke through. 'If I was breaking in, I wouldn't be dumb enough to do it in broad daylight. I've rented the apartment from them.'

'Oh.' Neil was startled. They'd said nothing about renting the apartment in their house. It had been vacant for three months. But the Kendricks – even after seventeen years in Bentonville – had little communication with their neighbors.

'Mrs Kendrick gave me a key—' She was rummaging in her purse. 'But it won't work.' She held out the key.

'I'm sorry. I didn't know they were renting.' He was ingratiatingly apologetic. The Kendricks hadn't mentioned it because renting out apartments in private houses was against town ordinances, though they'd been guilty of this for years.

'I don't plan on spending the weekend in my car.' Her eyes were indignant. Beautiful blue eyes, he noted.

'Let me try the key.' He extended a hand.

'Sure.'

With grim determination he made several tries. She was right, he thought with approval, and returned the key. 'Whoever cut

30

the key stopped too soon.' He crossed to the window she'd tried to open, struggled for a few moments, then slid it up.

'Muscle power,' she applauded. 'Thank you.'

'I'll open the door for you.' He climbed through the window, moments later shoved the apartment door wide. 'Don't worry about leaving it open if you have to go out,' he told her. 'Nobody in town locks doors except at bedtime.'

'Thank you,' she said again with obvious relief. 'Oh, I'm Laurie Evans, new in town.'

'Welcome, Laurie Evans. I live across the street.' He waved a hand in the direction of his house. 'I'm Neil Winston.'

'I think it's great that you bothered to check that I wasn't breaking and entering. It backs up everything I've said about the advantages of living in a small town.'

So she's from a big city. Probably New York. 'If you encounter any more problems, just yell for help.' *What a gorgeous smile.* 'I was once an Eagle Scout.' *What brought Laurie Evans to this town? Is there a Mr Evans?*

Laurie stood in the doorway and watched Neil Winston cross the street. What was it about him that she found so attractive? His rugged good looks? Or the way he'd come charging over to protect his neighbors' house? Now she froze at attention. The door of his house had just swung open. She squinted nearsightedly. A woman stood there.

So he's married. What does that mean to me? I don't want a man in my life. They just complicate things. I know where I'm going – and I'll go there alone.

Four

Laurie focused on unloading the car. Perspiration dampened her forehead, caused her blouse to cling between her shoulderblades. Tim was right – people sweated in Bentonville, too. She was conscious of hunger as she deposited the last carton in a corner of her small living room. Unpack later. Walk into town and find a place where she could have lunch.

Oh, check to make sure the phone was connected. It was, she discovered with relief. Should she call Tim and Iris, let them know she'd arrived? Later, when the evening rates were in effect. Teachers' salaries were low. She was on a budget.

She made sure the front door remained unlocked when she left the house. Neil Winston said nobody in town locked their doors except at bedtime. Wow, who would dare do that in New York? That would be an open invitation to burglars.

In the hot early afternoon sun, she headed for Main Street. Down the block a cluster of early teens played ball. Across the street a

33

young woman sprayed two small boys with a hose while they screeched with delight. Would they be in her class? she wondered whimsically. They looked about eight.

She exchanged 'hello's with three women headed in the opposite direction. This would never happen in Manhattan, she thought with pleasure. She paused to pat a playful collie. One of these days she'd get herself a puppy.

On Main Street she spied a small restaurant – The Oasis, the window sign proclaimed. She went inside. It was typical of its kind, Laurie thought. It could have been in New York or Chicago or anywhere. But she admired the fresh flower in a small vase at each table. That was small-town. The restaurant was lightly populated at this hour – past the lunchtime rush. A smiling, middle-aged waitress came to her table.

'The day's sandwich special is roast beef, the soup is split pea.' The waitress handed her a menu. 'You want a few minutes to look?'

'I'm starving,' Laurie said ebulliently. 'Roast beef on rye toast, please, and ice tea.'

'Coming right up,' the waitress promised, retrieving the menu. 'Ain't this a scorcher? I'll bring your ice tea right away.'

She ate with gusto, warned herself not to dawdle, though the ceiling fans in the restaurant provided some relief from the heat. She should do all the unpacking before dinner. After dinner – once the dishes were out of the way – she'd settle down to start reading the George Orwell book – *Nineteen Eighty-Four* – which she'd been meaning to read since it came out the year before but never seemed to find the time. Tim said you had to sit down and read it over a long weekend.

'But I warn you, it's a grim prediction of a totalitarian state.'

On the way home she picked up groceries at the A&P she'd noticed at the end of Main Street. Just a few things to see her through until tomorrow. In the morning she'd drive to the A&P and load up the car. Oh, pick up a newspaper. Mrs Kendrick told her there was the *Enquirer* in the morning and the *Record* in the late afternoon.

She chatted with the cashier about the weather when she paid her check. A refugee from Germany, she surmised from the cashier's accented English. A small, slender woman of about thirty-five. Such a warm, charming smile, but the eyes were so sad. She remembered the clusters of German refugees that used to gather in the cafeterias on the Upper West Side in New York. She'd felt such compassion for them. Could Americans ever truly realize how lucky they were?

Back at her apartment she prodded herself

into the unpacking chore. How had she managed to get so much in a few cartons? But at last the unpacking was done, clothes hung away, dresser drawers neatly filled. She plugged in the television set, manipulated the 'rabbit ears' antenna until she could get decent reception.

For dinner she settled for a cheese omelet and fresh string beans, with an apple for dessert. After dinner she watched a few minutes of the evening news. More craziness about the House Un-American Activities Committee hearings, she condemned in distaste, and flipped off the television.

She and Tim and Iris had spent many frustrated hours bemoaning what was happening in Washington, the way the 'Hollywood Ten' had been sentenced to jail terms last month. Careers were being destroyed on the strength of rumors. But that was all far away from a serene small town like Bentonville.

She checked her watch. Still too early to call Tim and Iris. She reached for the copy of the *Enquirer*, which she'd picked up at the candy store. Her eyes widened in pleasure as she read about the presence of the Bentonville Arts League. So much for Tim's warning that Bentonville would be devoid of cultural events. *'You love going to concerts and the theater and the museums. The big deal in Bentonville will be a Saturday night at the drive-in.*'

There were to be four performances – to be held at the high school auditorium. The first featured Boris Kerensky. He was the pianist who had defected from Russia, Laurie recalled, and lived now in Philadelphia. She'd heard him on records. He was wonderful. She must go to this concert.

She read the Friday edition of the *Enquirer* from cover to cover. So it wasn't the *New York Times*, she thought defensively. It reported on national and world events more fully than most small-town newspapers. And she enjoyed its small town aura, too. Only now did she recall that Mrs Kendrick had spoken of the *Enquirer* with a disparaging tone. Too liberal a newspaper for her taste, Laurie interpreted. Mrs Kendrick read the *Record*. Probably the local ultra-conservative newspaper.

Earlier than anticipated – after she'd talked by phone with Tim and Iris – Laurie abandoned reading the George Orwell book, prepared for bed. She was tired. The excitement of the day, she told herself. But again sleep was slow in coming. A fan would be helpful – but this late in the year should she bother? The cost of the car had been a huge drain on her savings. This was budget time.

Kicking off the top sheet, she was conscious of the sweet scent of flowers that drifted into her small bedroom. Somewhere in the distance frogs frolicked noisily. Her low chuckle interrupted the night quiet as she remembered the time she had complained as a ten-year-old – when they were living somewhere in Asia – that the frogs were keeping her awake. That was after a two-year stretch of living in the heart of Paris.

In the morning she awoke with an instant awareness of being in a strange bed, a strange town. Birds chirped just outside her bedroom windows. The beguiling scent of roses permeated the air.

No raucous sounds of a garbage truck on its morning rounds. No shrill fire trucks or ambulances rushing to their destinations. No impatient drivers leaning on horns. This was a small piece of heaven.

That was Laurie's unwary assessment on this Saturday morning of the Labor Day weekend.

After breakfast Laurie left the apartment – remembering that the front door must remain unlocked – to head for the A&P to shop for groceries. A faint breeze helped to alleviate yesterday's near-record-breaking heat. Approaching the car she spied Neil pulling a lawn mower from the garage. He saw her, waved, appeared to be about to come over. She waved back, hurried into the car. Don't encourage him.

There was the usual Saturday morning crowd at the A&P. Her wagon loaded, she joined the line at a checkout counter. The apartment was all right for now, she considered – but one day she'd like to have a small house that she could decorate to her own taste.

'Joey, no candy!' a young mother screeched at a four-year-old making a grab for a chocolate bar near the register. 'You know what the dentist said!'

A single woman would never be allowed to adopt, Laurie thought wistfully. But then in time she'd have a niece or nephew – or both – to spoil. But no man in her life, she warned herself yet again.

She'd promised herself this long weekend would be a small vacation. She'd worked part-time all through the college years, fulltime this past summer – to beef up her savings. She'd bought an armful of paperbacks in a glorious splurge. At 25¢ and 35¢ a book, how could she not indulge herself?

After lunch she dragged the chaise the Kendricks had provided onto the porch, settled herself with the Orwell book. In a matter of minutes she discarded this as too heavy reading for such a glorious day. She was content to lie back on the chaise and relax. In moments she was asleep.

Well over an hour later she awoke to the

sound of firecrackers. Exuberant young voices floated from down the street as the late morning was punctuated by the raucous sound of fireworks. It was the Labor Day weekend – kids grasped at any holiday to bring out the fireworks, she forgave this intrusion.

She spied Neil Winston again. He was pulling a barbecue grill from the driveway and around to the back of the house. So he and his wife were having a cook-out this evening. It was a perfect night for that. They had no kids, she surmised. No indications of that.

She debated about going inside to prepare a lunch tray. Another ten minutes of loafing, she decided. It was so pleasant just to lie here on the porch. But she tensed as she saw Neil crossing from his house in her direction.

'Hi.' His smile was warm – too admiring for a married man, she thought in annoyance. 'The heatwave's broken.'

'Thank heaven for that.' Her voice was guarded.

'We're having a cook-out tonight. Just a few friends. I thought you might like to join us.'

'Thanks so much, but I'm just exhausted from getting settled in. And I still have unpacking ahead of me.' This was a small-town thing to do, she thought self-consciously –

to invite a neighbor for a cook-out.

'Another time then.' But his eyes told her he was disappointed by her rejection. 'If you encounter any problems give a holler.'

'Thanks.' It was difficult not to respond to his friendly puppy approach. 'I'll probably sleep away the whole weekend.'

Now she went into the house to prepare lunch. It was 'small town friendly' of him to invite her to their cook-out, Laurie acknowledged. But the way he looked at her made her wary. His wife wouldn't have been happy about that.

She moved through the rest of the day in a casual haze. She'd have an early dinner, then settle down to watch television. She'd bought the set just a few months ago at Tim's prodding. *'Hey, get with the times. It's the next big scene.'* And she must write a letter to Eve, down in Atlanta – give Eve her new address and phone number.

As she prepared her own dinner, she was aware of delicious aromas of hamburgers grilling over charcoal, heard the convivial sounds of the Winstons' small party. All at once conscious of her alone-ness, she abandoned the prospect of dining at the tiny table in her kitchen. She found a tray in a kitchen cabinet, carried her dinner plate and glass of ice tea into the living room. A television program would be her dinner companion.

41

Earlier than anticipated she began to fight off yawns. She dozed intermittently through a comedy program, concluded it was time to retire. It was this wonderful fresh air, she told herself. The lovely small-town quiet.

She slept late on Sunday morning, headed for Main Street after breakfast to pick up the Sunday newspapers. Not likely she'd be able to find a copy of the *New York Times*, she thought subconsciously. Still, arriving at the newsstand she glanced about to see if the Sunday *Times* was available. It wasn't.

She picked up copies of the Sunday *Enquirer* and the Sunday *Record*, walked inside to pay the middle-aged man behind the counter. He lifted an eyebrow and grinned. 'You'll be reading the *Enquirer* and the *Record*,' he commented with a quizzical grin. 'You must be new in town.'

'That's right.' She relished his totally friendly attitude. It confirmed her feelings about small town living. 'I'll be teaching at the elementary school.'

'We've got a good school here,' he bragged. 'All three of my kids went on to college. Course, the girl got married three months after graduation.'

Laurie assumed that meant the end of his daughter's career – whatever it was meant to be. But there were others like herself, she remembered defensively. On the ship

42

coming home from Italy her WAC group had talked about the future. Sure, some girls would be willing to settle down to the housewife routine. But others were as determined as she to build careers.

She was aware of the Sunday-morning atmosphere as she returned to her apartment. Long lines of cars surrounded the two churches that she passed – testament that this was, indeed, a church-going town. She heard – somewhere out of sight – the exuberant sounds of a baseball game in progress. She felt a surge of well-being. Oh yes, she'd done well to come to Bentonville.

Sunday was a lazy day – spent perusing the pages of both the Sunday *Enquirer* and the Sunday *Record*. Clearly they were on opposite sides on the question of the town's approving the construction of a large shopping center at the edge of town. The *Enquirer* worried about the fate of Main Street if residents were lured away to the newness of a shopping center, warned what had happened in other towns when shopping centers moved in. The *Record* praised the increased tax revenue the shopping center was sure to provide.

She made a self-conscious effort to avoid lounging on the porch. Now she felt guilty at rejecting yesterday's invitation to the cook-out. It had been just a warm, neighborly gesture, she reproached herself. She'd read an absurd message in Neil Winston's eyes.

On Monday morning she saw a gray Chevy emerge from the Winstons' garage – Neil at the wheel. Then Mrs Winston hurried from the house with a hamper in tow. They were probably headed for a picnic or a day at the lake a few miles out of town, Laurie surmised. On Saturday morning, she recalled, Tim and Iris had left to spend the weekend at a borrowed cottage on Fire Island. For the first time she felt a twinge of homesickness.

Determined to fill the empty hours she focused on going through her wardrobe, making sure clothes were in shape for the rest of the week. Tomorrow there was the meeting at the school. On Wednesday classes began.

Late in the afternoon the gray Chevy returned. She spied Nail hanging a swimsuit, a pair of swimming trunks, and towels on a clothesline that extended across the back of their property. They'd gone to spend the day at the lake, she surmised.

Early in the evening – while she ate her dinner before the television set – she heard a car pull up in the driveway. She left her chair to peer out the window. In the dwindling daylight she saw the short, obese figure of Maisie Kendrick emerge from the car. Then her husband, Bud – a scrawny little man with a perpetual stoop – was at the trunk. In the morning, Laurie decided, she'd ask for a working key. A nice quiet couple, she thought, returning to her chair and dinner tray. But that assessment was obliterated half an hour later while she washed her dishes in the kitchen sink.

'Why can't you do anything right?' Maisie Kendrick screeched. 'Why do I have to do everything? You're the man! I'm not supposed to have to remember to bring along water in case the car overheats! If you were worth a damn, you'd be making money to buy a new car by now!'

'Stop your goddamn whining!' her husband yelled. 'That's all you ever do – complain, complain, complain!'

Laurie felt herself an unwilling intruder as the battle between the two in the other part of the house raged on until he slammed out of the house. To head for a neighborhood bar, Laurie assumed from his wife's parting accusation.

On Tuesday morning – with Mrs Kendrick having promised to leave a working key on her dining table later in the morning – Laurie left her apartment with a sense of adventure. There was to be a half-day general meeting of the staff of all twelve grades. After that they would meet in smaller groups, broken down by grades. How wonderful to be able to walk to school,

45

she rejoiced. No shoving her way into a crowded subway or bus.

She was relieved that she'd heard no angry fighting in the other part of the house this morning. They'd seemed so pleasant, almost reticent when she'd met them earlier. But what happened in the privacy of their home was none of her business, she told herself.

She approached the school with anticipation. Large for a town this size, she thought, viewing the sprawling two-story red-brick structure. The original wing housed the first eight grades. The added wing contained the high school classrooms and offices, the auditorium and the gym. A sprinkling of cars indicated that some of the staff lived at a distance – or were reluctant to undertake lengthy walks.

She was conscious of friendly stares from a pair of women approaching the entrance along with her. She was the only new teacher joining the staff this year.

'It's a gorgeous morning, isn't it?' The younger of the women – probably in her late-twenties – greeted Laurie with candid curiosity.

'Beautiful,' Laurie agreed.

'You're the new third grade teacher?'

'That's right. Laurie Evans.'

'I'm Pat Logan, fourth grade – and this is Sharon Jackson, first grade.'

'Welcome, Laurie.' Sharon Jackson was

about twenty years Pat's senior, Laurie guessed. No doubt a veteran in the Bentonville school system. 'I hope you stay with us longer than the last two third grade teachers.'

'What happened to the last two?' Laurie asked.

'The last one left to get married.' Pat uttered an elaborate sigh. 'It should happen to me. And the teacher before her left to join the WACs.'

'She didn't return to teaching?' All at once Laurie felt a touch of wariness – remembering that WACs were not regarded with approval by some in this country.

'Oh, she wanted to come back,' Sharon Jackson said with a hint of distaste. 'But of course, the School Board wouldn't hear of it. If she deserted the school at a time when it was losing several men teachers, why should she be welcomed back?'

Thank God, Laurie thought with relief, that she hadn't mentioned her seventeen months with the WACs on her application for the teaching position.

Pat and Sharon indicated that they were to gather first in the auditorium for an address by the principal. Laurie was impressed by the size of the staff. But of course, the one school served the entire town with the exception of students who attended the local parochial school.

There was much good-humored exchange of conversation among the gathering. Either Pat or Sharon made a point of introducing her to others.

'Mr Franklin can be kind of long-winded,' Pat whispered. 'But he's not a bad guy.'

'He's heading for the stage now,' Sharon pointed out and turned around in her seat to inspect the entrance. 'They'll be closing the doors in a minute. Oh, he just made it in time,' she said indulgently.

'Who?' Pat asked and also turned towards the entrance.

'Neil Winston,' Sharon said and Laurie swerved about to view the newcomer.

'He and his wife life across the way from me,' Laurie told them, struggling to sound casual. *He's a teacher.* 'I have an apartment in the Kendricks' house.'

'Oh, Neil isn't married,' Pat said. 'He lives with his mother. Of course, Doris Lowell keeps trying.' Pat giggled. 'And she's not the only one.'

Laurie was conscious of the sudden pounding of her heart. The 'we' to whom he'd referred when he'd invited her to their cook-out was himself and his mother.

But why should that concern me? I'm not in pursuit of Neil Winston.

Five

As Pat had warned, Mr Franklin was long-winded. From the expressive exchanges between Pat and Sharon, Laurie gathered that much of what he said had been heard in earlier years. But at last Mr Franklin was listing the room numbers for the group meetings. Now he dismissed the gathering.

'We have two assistant principals, but Franklin had no intention of letting them speak,' Sharon whispered. 'He wants to be sure everybody understands he's in charge.' Even here, Laurie realized reluctantly, there was a battle for power.

'We'll point you in the right direction,' Pat bubbled as they headed up the clogged aisle of the auditorium.

The atmosphere was almost convivial, Laurie thought. Everybody glad to be back in harness after the summer vacation. Involuntarily her eyes wandered in search of Neil Winston. What grade did he teach? Not that it mattered to her.

'I wonder if Neil plans on having a debating group again this year?' Sharon said. 'I told my nephew Luke to be sure to join up if he does.'

'How old is Luke now?' Pat asked.

'He'll be sixteen in December.' So Neil teaches high school, Laurie decided. 'He's real interested in politics – and you know how folks in town keep saying that Neil will probably run for office one of these days. That could be a great contact for Luke.'

'We never would have gotten the new equipment for the gym nor the extension for the public library if he hadn't gone out and fought for them. And he arranged – and raised the funds – for the school trip down to New York last spring,' Pat told Laurie. 'That one's a fighter.'

The meeting of the third grade teachers lasted slightly over an hour before dissolving into personal conversation. Laurie emerged with a sense of satisfaction. She liked the approach of the three other third grade teachers, shared most of their ideas about how to approach individual subjects. And how wonderful, she thought with appreciation, that the class size was limited to twenty-two students.

'We can call it a day now,' one teacher decided in high spirits. 'We'll be back in the old grind tomorrow. And welcome to the fold, Laurie.'

In the lobby Laurie encountered Pat.

'You've been initiated.' Pat grinned. 'We

gripe regularly, but this is a great school.'

'Hi!' Neil approached Laurie and Pat, turned with mock reproach to Laurie. 'You didn't tell me you were our new third grade teacher.'

'You didn't tell me you were a teacher,' Laurie flipped. 'What subject?'

'English. That means I get stuck with running a debating group and the dramatic groups.' He sighed eloquently.

'You love it, Neil.' Pat turned to Laurie. 'This guy has a real fan club among the students. Of course, it doesn't hurt that he's real good-looking.'

'Neil!' A feminine voice called out. 'I've been looking all over for you.' A tall blonde with a petulant smile joined them.

'Doris Lowell,' Pat whispered with an edge of sarcasm.

'Hi, Doris.' Neil's smile was wary. Laurie remembered Pat's comment about her chasing after Neil.

'Did you hear who the concert committee booked for the first of the season?' Doris radiated disapproval.

'Boris Kerensky.' Laurie's voice was reverent. 'He's marvelous.'

'But not his politics,' Doris clucked.

'Laurie, this is Doris Lowell. Laurie Evans,' Neil introduced them.

'What about this guy's politics?' Pat was curious. 'Not that I get involved with such

51

things.'

'Well, he's Russian, isn't he?' Doris looked at Neil for back-up. 'You'd think the committee would consider that before booking him. I mean, you know all the talk about Commies these days.'

'I don't think Boris Kerensky will contaminate the school by playing the piano in the high school auditorium,' Laurie chided lightly. 'It's like saying we shouldn't have Russian dressing on our salads.'

Doris stiffened, turned to Neil. 'Remember the concerts last year? You thought they were all marvelous.' The implication being, Laurie thought, that Doris Lowell had attended the concerts with Neil. 'All of them were American artists.'

'They'd hoped to bring in Jascha Heifitz, but this town couldn't afford his fee,' Neil recalled. His face brightened at the sight of a woman – broom and dustpan in hand – crossing to a small pile of debris in a corner of the lobby. A colored woman in her late-fifties, Laurie noted, and was suddenly aware that this was the first colored person she'd seen in Bentonville. 'How're you doing, Beverly?' he called out.

The woman looked up, smiled. 'Jes' fine, Mist' Winston. I missed seein' you during school vacation.'

'You make sure Bobby starts school tomorrow,' he urged. 'I had a long talk with

52

him a couple of days ago.'

'Oh, he'll be there for sure.' She lifted a hand in a small gesture of farewell.

'Beverly is part of our janitorial help,' Neil told Laurie. 'She's been raising her grandson since his mother died some years ago. He dropped out last year to go to work when she was laid up with a broken leg. But he's a bright kid – it's important he get through high school.'

'That's Neil for you,' Doris drawled, a possessive note in her voice that was making him uncomfortable. 'Always worried about some student or other.'

'I'd better run.' Neil's smile was rueful. 'My car's making strange noises – I want Dave at the garage to have a look at it.' He waved in farewell as he headed for the door.

'Thwarted again,' Pat drawled. 'She never gives up.'

'Let's go somewhere for a sandwich and coffee,' Sharon suggested. 'Our last day of freedom.'

'Teaching isn't that bad,' Laurie protested. 'But yes, I'd like a sandwich and coffee.'

On Wednesday morning Laurie walked into her classroom with a blend of trepidation and exhilaration. This wasn't student teaching. She was on her own. But how intimidating could twenty-two third-graders be? She considered her plans for the first day,

53

once again perused the list of students. They were probably full of misgivings, too. They were about to meet a new teacher for the first time.

A small fair-haired boy walked shyly into the room. He smiled. Laurie smiled back.

'Good morning,' she said softly. 'I'm Miss Evans, your teacher. And what's your name?'

'David Kahn.' He was walking towards a front chair. 'Is it all right if I sit up front?' A faint accent in his voice. German?

'Please do sit up front,' Laurie urged. She remembered the friendly cashier with sad eyes at The Oasis – where she'd had lunch on her arrival in town. Her son?

Speaking with David had set her at ease, Laurie realized. The day would go well.

She was charmed by the cluster of eight-year-olds who walked into the room with varying degrees of diffidence, knew instantly which was the bully of the class. She was conscious of the varied personalities. It would be a challenge to reach them, she told herself – but one she welcomed.

At lunch time she joined the line at the school cafeteria, carried her tray into the elementary teachers' lunchroom. Pat beckoned her to the table she shared with Sharon and another teacher.

'You're surviving,' Pat effervesced as Laurie took her seat at the table for four, introduced Laurie to Karen Goldberg, who taught fifth grade. A warm, friendly woman of about thirty, Laurie guessed – and liked her on sight. 'The first hour is the worst.'

Over lunch Laurie became aware of undercurrents in the school. There was a strong division between the elementary teachers, most of whom were women.

'It's weird,' Karen Goldberg scoffed. 'We've got teachers who are scared to death of everything Russian.' Laurie remembered Doris Lowell – a member of that group. 'I think about my Russian immigrant grandparents and wonder how they'd survive in this town if they were alive.'

'All those jerks think about,' Sharon began, then glanced about and lowered her voice, 'is that Russia has three times as many fighter planes as we have, four times as many troops. And they remember Russia exploded an atomic bomb last year. If they could afford it, they'd all be building bomb shelters under their houses.'

'This isn't a lunch-time topic.' Pat grunted in disapproval. 'What's good on television this week? I've had my fill of Milton Berle, Arthur Godfrey and *Gangbusters*.'

'We don't have television yet,' Sharon admitted. 'Though my father's hinting that it's coming soon. He's bored now that he's retired. Too many empty hours. He figures with television in the house he can watch all the sports events and the news.' Sharon chuckled. 'He thinks it might wean my mother from her radio soap operas. I told him not to bet on that. If she broke her leg, she'd want to be carried home so she could hear *Guiding Light* and *The Romance of Helen Trent*.'

Pat giggled. 'The soaps will be coming to TV soon. Wait and see. I hear there's one scheduled to start any day now.'

'Howie says we ought to volunteer to work for the Democratic Club's candidates for Town Council,' Karen said. Her husband, Laurie assumed. 'Though the chances of their getting in are slim. But we do need more funds for the school system, and only the Democrats will fight for that.'

'Who's going to vote for higher property taxes?' Sharon shook her head. 'Not my father. Or anybody else I know.'

'Howie and I will vote for it,' Karen said with a touch of defiance. 'I should think any family with children will. And what about you?' she challenged Pat.

'Oh, I never bother voting. My mother never did either.' Pat shrugged this off.

Laurie was shocked. 'How can you not vote?'

'Easy. I don't go to the polls. I can't be bothered. So it's two less votes. That's not going to make a difference.'

'But how many other women feel that

way?' Laurie stared in disbelief. 'Women's votes – if they vote – can throw an election in the right direction.' It took so many years for women to get the vote in this country, Laurie fumed in silence – but women like Pat and her mother couldn't be bothered.

'My father would kill me if I voted for higher property taxes,' Pat said. 'He complains about taxes now.'

The five-minute warning bell sounded. There was the clatter of dishes as teachers loaded their trays, prepared to clear their tables and return to the classrooms.

Laurie gazed each morning at the parade of cars that rolled into the parking area of the school grounds with recurrent astonishment. Were she and Neil the only teachers who walked to school? But then Pat told her that since the end of the war folks were moving away from downtown.

'You know, with all the couples who were getting married when the guys came back from the war, they had to build new houses.' A bitterness in Pat's voice that Sharon had explained later.

'Pat had been writing to this boy for almost three years. He enlisted right after Pearl Harbor. They'd been in high school together, then both were at the same college. Folks expected them to get married once they were out of school. He was stationed in England, was part of the D-Day invasion, the liberation of Paris. But in Paris he met a girl.' Sharon's eyes had glowed with contempt. 'A month before he came home, he wrote Pat that he was getting married – to this French girl.'

Why did Pat think it was the end of the world to be single? Laurie asked herself as she swigged down a second cup of coffee before heading for school this first day of her second week of teaching. They'd gone to the drive-in movie at the edge of town on Saturday to see *Father of the Bride*, and Pat had made cracks about two girls going to a drive-in together. As though they should be ashamed not to have a Saturday-night date. Pat was dreading her birthday next month. *'God, I can't believe I'm going to be thirty!'* Her flippant air of amusement seemed to disguise something close to panic. *'My mother's sure I'll never get married. My kid sister has been married for almost six years – she's got two kids.'*

Yesterday for the first time Laurie felt a real twinge of homesickness. On weekends in New York there was always something interesting to do. But she brushed this aside. She awoke each morning to blessed quiet. She looked out her bedroom window to see flowers in bloom, birds flitting through the trees. She walked to school instead of fighting her way into a subway car packed with humanity.

She'd go down to New York to spend the long Thanksgiving holiday with Tim and Iris, she plotted as she left her apartment this morning. Across the way she saw Neil emerge from his house. So this morning he wasn't going in so early. She saw him gaze across at her. He waved. She waved back. Was he coming over here? To walk to school with her? On sudden impulse, she strode to her car, her heart pounding. She'd drive this morning. No room in her life for Neil Winston. No room in her life for any man.

Six

Life was settling into a comfortable pattern, Laurie told herself with subconscious bravado at the end of her third week in town. She loved the serenity of Bentonville. So every once in a while the quiet of the house was destroyed by the shriek-filled battles between the Kendricks. She was living the kind of life she'd dreamed about.

She closed her eyes to conflict over the issue of raising property taxes to improve the schools. So a handful of local people were uptight about the Red Scare. Most barely knew what was happening with the House Un-American Activities Committee. They'd never heard of *Red Channels*. They were more involved in their personal problems. Could they afford a new car this year? Was their twelve-year-old going to need braces?

She saw Neil only at a distance at school. He ate lunch in the high school teachers' lunchroom. From her apartment she saw him heading for school most mornings, a solid half-hour before she left. Something to do with his special groups, she surmised. And it disturbed her that he invaded her thoughts at unwary intervals.

Weekends were 'catch-up' time. She shopped for groceries, cleaned the apartment, did laundry, washed her hair. Saturday evenings she went to the drive-in with Pat. On Sundays she tried to relax with the two local newspapers plus the Sunday *New York Times*, which her news dealer acquired for her, along with two other customers.

At unwary moments she was conscious of Neil's activities across the way. He mowed their lawn – probably for the last time this year, she guessed. He was repairing the picket fence across the front of their house. She was terrified when she saw him atop the roof, doing something with the chimney – relieved when she saw him on solid ground again.

On an unseasonably cool Sunday she caught the scent of birch logs burning in the fireplace. Of course, Neil would be the type who enjoyed a blazing fire in the fireplace grate.

She was concerned that the Town Council might not pass the measure to provide more money for the school system. How could someone as nice as Pat Logan not go to the polls in November to vote for it? Pat knew the schools were operating under a painful handicap. But there were others, like Karen and her husband, who would vote the rise in school taxes.

She'd learned from Pat that Karen had been teaching in the Bentonville school system for just two years. She and her husband – a lawyer – had moved here from New York City. They, too, were newcomers, she thought with pleasure. She'd volunteer to work for the Democratic candidates, she decided. That was the way to meet people, to become part of the town.

The *Enquirer* was giving much space to the coming elections, Laurie noted. They supported the Democratic candidates. She remembered what Sharon said about the *Enquirer*: 'It's a far better newspaper than the *Record*, but its circulation is forty per cent less. The *Record* is owned by Cliff Rogers and he has definite ideas about how this town should be run. Most of them good for a handful of folks in this town, including himself.'

Laurie's thoughts focused on Neil. She'd take any bets that he'd vote for providing more money for the schools. Of course, Tim would scold her for making snap decisions about people. She could hear his voice now:

'Laurie, when the hell are you going to stop acting like an impulsive little kid? Always jumping to quick conclusions about people. Remember when you were sure that women who lived across the road from us was the nicest mother in

the world – and then she drowned her two-year-old in the bathtub?'

But that was when she was eleven.

On Friday afternoon of her fourth week in Bentonville little David Kahn shyly approached her at the conclusion of class. He had questions about their assignment.

'But, David, you'll miss your bus,' she hesitated.

'I walk home,' he explained. 'We live right near. I just wondered about—'

'Your mother won't worry if you're late getting home?'

'She works at The Oasis,' he explained. 'She won't be home till four o'clock.' His mother was the charming cashier with the German accent, Laurie realized, and felt a rush of sympathy. David and his mother must be refugees from the Holocaust.

'Come sit right down, and I'll go over the assignment with you.' What a bright little boy, she thought – and remembered Pat's complaint about a little girl in her class. *'God, that kid never stops asking questions. How does her mother stand her?'* Pat admitted she'd gone into teaching because her parents thought it was a 'nice, ladylike profession'.

With David's questions answered, he left the classroom, his smile confident. Laurie packed her tote with books she wanted to look over in the course of the weekend and

63

left her classroom. Approaching the front entrance she encountered Karen Goldberg.

'Hi, how're you doing?'

'Good. I have a great bunch of kids.' Laurie paused. 'A couple of problem ones, but I guess that's routine.'

'Why don't we run over to The Oasis for coffee and gab? I just learned that you're from New York City, too.'

'Sure.' Laurie's smile was bright. She welcomed some socializing. Pat had suggested they go to the drive-in movie Sunday night and she'd agreed. Saturday night Pat was going to a baby shower. 'I spent four years at Hunter, then went to Columbia for my graduate degree.'

'Howie – my husband – went to Columbia Law.' *He was probably there at the same time as Phil.* 'But he knew he'd never be happy working for some huge law firm. He wasn't interested in corporate law. He wanted to defend people with little money but who desperately needed help.' Karen chuckled. 'He'll never make a lot of money, but we'll always manage. And he'll be one of those rare people who're happy with what they're doing.'

'That's being rich,' Laurie said softly.

'He always knew he wanted to be a lawyer. He went to law school straight out of the army. I was teaching in the Bronx.' Karen and Laurie left the building in companionable silence for a moment. 'How did you come to decide on Bentonville as a place to live?'

'Oh, I got in my car and drove all around this area. I wanted out of New York in the worst way,' Laurie admitted. 'Then I saw Bentonville – it's such a pretty town. And about the right size, I thought, for easy living. I came back and looked around – and decided this was it.'

'Howie was in service with a very sweet guy from Bentonville. He never stopped talking about it.' All at once Karen was somber. 'He didn't make it back. I think Howie felt he was coming back here for Jeff.'

'My father was in the diplomatic service – we roamed around the globe when I was growing up. I kept longing to settle somewhere. So at last I've set down roots.'

'Of course, we'll live here twenty-five years, and we'll still be outsiders,' Karen warned. 'That's the small-town syndrome.'

Laurie was startled. This didn't fit her vision of small-town living.

'But you have a chance,' she teased. 'Marry a local boy whose family has lived here for three or four generations. Then you'll be one of them.'

'But everybody – almost everybody – is so friendly.'

'Sure – but we're still outsiders. We know

a few people who weren't born here. When we get together,' Karen reminisced, a hint of laughter in her eyes, 'it feels almost like a meeting of an expatriate society.'

At The Oasis Laurie and Karen sat at a rear corner table. The restaurant was lightly populated, as on the day she arrived in town, Laurie recalled. The same cashier was on duty.

'I have a little boy – a darling child – in my class,' Laurie told Karen. 'I suspect the cashier here is his mother.'

Karen nodded. 'Sophie Kahn is as nice as she can be. She came here from New York, I gather – about three years ago. As you've probably realized, they're from Germany. I understand some German couple in a small town about a hundred miles north of Berlin hid Sophie and her son until the end of the war. Her husband died in a concentration camp.'

'There were good people everywhere during the war—' Laurie paused as a waitress came to their table to take their orders. When the waitress left, she resumed her thought. 'I remember in Italy – in this little village where we were stationed for several weeks—' She paused again at Karen's avid stare. 'I spent seventeen months as a WAC. I haven't mentioned that to anybody here – not even on my teacher's application.'

'That I can understand.'

66

'We heard stories about how when Hitler rounded up Italian Jews and sent them to Auschwitz, there were simple Italian farmers who managed to hide Jewish neighbors until it was safe for them to emerge.'

'I grew up in New York City. If there was anti-Semitism, I never felt it personally – though we all knew that the telephone company never hired Jews, that there were quotas at colleges – including Columbia.'

'I went to Columbia for my master's.' Laurie was taken aback. 'There were Jewish students—'

'Within the quota,' Karen pointed out. 'Then I visited the state of North Carolina.' Karen's face tensed. 'I was teaching already, so when school closed for the summer I decided to raid my savings and go down for a month to be near Howie. He enlisted a week after we were secretly married. We knew it was a matter of time before he'd be drafted. Anyhow, he was stationed down in North Carolina, and I went traipsing down to this small town down there to be near when he had time off from the base. I used my single name – Karen Miller – when I went searching for a furnished room. No sweat to find one. Then Howie came to the boarding house – and I introduced him to my landlady. "This is my husband, Howard Goldberg." And the next day she told me to get out. "We don't rent to no Jews."' Karen shrugged. 'In the good old USA – in the middle of the war.'

'I wasn't happy with what I knew personally about the way the colored WACs were treated in the war years.' Laurie grimaced eloquently. 'But that's changing. Barriers are beginning to come down.'

'We've got a long way to go,' Karen warned.

'There must be very few colored families in town. The only colored person I've seen is the woman janitor at the school. But what about the student body?' Laurie asked.

'A total of fourteen colored students from kindergarten through twelfth grade. Colored families are slow to settle in small towns.'

'Twenty years from now,' Laurie predicted, 'we'll see a totally different world.'

Laurie's mind traveled back to the letter she'd received from Eve. She'd worried about Eve's traveling into a segregated schools area. As a colored student in New York Eve had never encountered segregated classes. Like herself, Eve was so pleased by President Truman's stand on civil rights. Right now the army was in the process of being desegregated.

But she remembered Eve's description of the colored school where she was teaching. *'Laurie, you wouldn't believe the situation here. I'm teaching in a one-room school house – with no electricity, no running water.'*

In the enlightened year of 1950 this was happening in the South.

In the cheery Winston kitchen Beth Winston poured a second cup of coffee for her son and herself.

'You aren't coming down with something, Neil?' Beth was solicitous. 'You're so quiet this morning.'

'No,' Neil denied guiltily. He couldn't admit his thoughts were dominated by their new neighbor. Was he imagining that Laurie Evans was avoiding him? Now he realized his mother was expecting further explanation. 'I've been trying to figure out how to handle a problem at school. You know how stuffy Carl Franklin can be sometimes.'

'Oh, I know.' She clucked in distaste. 'I remember when he came into the book store and tried to convince Eric to ban *Forever Amber* from the shop.' Beth Winston had clerked in the book store since her husband died sixteen years earlier – at a tragically young age.

'The mother of one of my seniors complained because I put that new hit novel about Hollywood – by Budd Schulberg – on my reading list.'

'*Disenchanted*? I loved it.'

'Anyhow, Franklin claims this mother said it's too much for her son's tender years. And I think Franklin agrees,' Neil conceded.

'Don't they realize that the kids in my senior class will – most of them – be eighteen this year, and the government says they have to register for the draft? They can fight a war – but they can't read *Disenchanted*!'

'What are you going to do?' Beth glanced at her watch, swigged down the last of her coffee. Neil was aware that his mother was always incensed at anything that hinted at censorship.

'I'll have to explain that they don't have to make that specific book their choice.' In a corner of his mind he remembered Laurie Evans' reaction to Doris's insinuations about Boris Kerensky. 'Sometimes, Mom, it's better to work around a problem like that than to explode.'

'I'd better get to the shop or Eric will explode.' Beth pushed back her chair. 'He wants me to call up some people about specific orders that have arrived.'

'Why can't Eric call them?' he reproached, then smiled sympathetically. 'I know, he's gotten very reclusive since those creepy kids scrawled "pansy" across the shop window.'

'Eric Hunter is one of the sweetest boys I know.' Beth chuckled. 'All right, he hasn't been a boy for quite a while. But folks can be so nasty.'

'I told Eric to put *Disenchanted* in the shop window,' Neil said with a mischievous smile.

'It's there.' Beth prepared to leave. 'How

do you feel about salmon, baked potato, and a salad for dinner?'

'Sounds great to me.'

Alone, Neil left the table to gaze out a kitchen window. Laurie's car sat in the driveway. Last Saturday he'd seen her leave the house in her car and return about an hour later with brown paper bags of groceries. A Saturday morning trip to the A&P, which would probably be repeated this morning, he surmised.

So she turned down his invitation to their cook-out – so she was tired, needed time to settle into her apartment. That didn't mean she was brushing him off. He reached for a pocket of his shirt. The tickets for the Kerensky concert were there. He'd walk over to the A&P, pick up some small item. He'd find her, go over and talk to her, offer to carry her groceries to the car. Of course, she'd offer him a ride home.

In his mind he rehearsed what he'd say. He'd casually invite her to go to the concert with him. *'I remember you said you love Boris Kerensky.'* Recalling their encounter the day of the staff meeting, he winced. Doris had a way of misrepresenting situations. He'd taken Doris to one concert last year – after being roped into it. He'd avoided any follow-up. In this town if you took a girl out just three times, you were considered engaged. He hadn't talked with Laurie since that day. Just a casual exchange of waves a few times.

He hated the jokes among the other teachers about how girl students had crushes on him. He loathed being pursued by several single teachers. Laurie Evans would never chase any man. You knew that just talking to her for a few minutes.

Why am I so drawn to Laurie? It's not just that she's so pretty. I like the way she thinks — the perky way she reacted when I thought she was breaking into the Kendricks' house. I even like the way she walks — quick, leaning forward slightly as though impatient to reach out to life. I've never felt this way about any girl.

The sound of a car starting up somewhere close punctured his reverie. He crossed to a window again. Laurie was backing out of her driveway. All right, head for the A&P.

Despite the heat of the morning Neil walked at a fast pace to the A&P. The parking area was loaded with cars. He spied Laurie's late-model Dodge. He'd been right about her destination.

Rumors said the supermarket was about to move to the edge of town, where they could expand the parking area. The three small independent grocery stores in town would appreciate that, he thought with sympathy.

Without bothering to take a shopping

cart, he joined the crush inside the sprawling supermarket. The usual Saturday morning hassle. Noisy, here and there a toddler outraged at the confines of the seat that was a standard part of the shopping cart, shoppers of all ages, though young couples seemed to predominate. Good-humored conversation as neighbors encountered one another.

Neil's eyes scanned first one aisle and then another. His face brightened. There she was, debating about what cereal to choose. From the contents of her shopping cart she'd soon be heading for the cash registers, he guessed with satisfaction. He pushed past other shoppers to join her.

'Hi, this is a popular destination this morning.'

She glanced up with a warm smile. 'We all have to eat. Unless we have suicidal intentions.'

'I noticed we were low on cereal. My mother said, "go shop".' He reached for a box. 'What a hot day, though.'

'The last gasp. In three months we'll be complaining about the cold.'

'Not me,' Neil chuckled. 'I love the cold. I remember during the war – going up all those mountains in Italy in the dead of winter I—'

'You were in Italy?' A strange excitement in her voice.

73

'I did the whole bit.' His eyes were reminiscent. 'North Africa, Sardinia, Sicily, Italy.'

'I missed North Africa, Sardinia, and Sicily, but I was in Italy,' Laurie said and stopped short. 'And not as a tourist.' She managed to sound simultaneously flip and defiant.

'You were an army nurse?' He was astonished – she seemed too young for that.

She hesitated a moment. 'I was a WAC.'

'You were probably right behind us!' He felt a surge of excitement. Laurie Evans *was* a special girl.

'I didn't mention serving in the WACs when I applied for the job at the school—' She hesitated, searching for words. 'Not everybody approved of us. Not even some of the soldiers. And back home a lot of people had the weird idea that we were there to entertain the troops. It wasn't like that,' she said grimly.

'Most of us over there knew that.' His mind dived into the past. 'I remember a group of six WACs who saved our hides many times when our equipment went down. They were the best damn mechanics any unit could want.'

'I was with the Signal corps,' Laurie said. 'We may not have been in the front lines according to the records, but we jumped into a lot of foxholes when the bombs starting falling. We did a good job.' She paused.

'When our captain discovered I spoke Italian, he drafted me as interpreter. That was exciting.'

'Let's get out of here and go some place where we can talk,' he said urgently. 'We might have been a few kilometers apart going up those mountains in Italy!'

'Remember those pinpoint turns?' Laurie shivered in recall. 'I used to close my eyes and pray.'

Caught up in the past they joined a line at the check-out counter – enveloped in the camaraderie of those who'd fought in the war. But for the moment they focused on casual talk.

'It's smart to be here early.' Laurie sighed with impatience. 'Why do I always remember that when I'm in a line on a Saturday morning?'

'The line's moving now,' Neil said, then groaned. A brawny male was pushing past them to dump an armload of cans into his wife's cart – just ahead of them.

With relief they left the supermarket – Neil carrying two of Laurie's loaded brown bags.

'Is your car here?' Laurie asked.

'No, I walked over. I knew I'd just have cereal to carry home.' Not exactly a lie, Neil thought, suppressing guilt.

'We could have coffee at my place,' Laurie said, eager to reminisce about the war years.

'Great,' he approved.

At the apartment Neil unpacked the parcels, put perishables into the refrigerator while Laurie handled the coffee making. With the percolator on the gas range they sat at the small dining table.

'How did you happen to go into the WACs?' Neil asked. 'I enlisted,' he conceded, 'because it was only a matter of time before I'd be drafted.'

'Actually I was there under false pretenses.' Her giggle was infectious. 'I was eighteen – twenty was the accepting age. But my brother – who was my legal guardian since our parents were killed in a plane crash two years earlier – was able to sign approval for me to join. I was a freshman at Hunter College down in New York. My closest friend had been talking about joining. For a while we thought we'd join together, but her parents insisted she stay in school. I signed up alone.' Laurie frowned. 'I'm glad she didn't enlist.'

'You're sorry you joined up?' He was startled. Not his image of Laurie Evans.

'Oh, no,' she rejected. 'I came out of the WACs feeling good about myself. But it would have been bad for Eve. She's colored.'

'I didn't know there were colored WACs,' he said in surprise. 'I guess I never thought about that—'

76

'Colored WACs got shameful treatment!' Laurie's eyes were blazing. 'Right from the start – at my Reception Center – I realized that. Many of the colored WACs had college degrees, but they were put to work scrubbing floors, cleaning latrines. In states where there was no segregation, colored WACs were assigned to "colored barracks", "colored sections" in the mess halls and classrooms. They weren't allowed to use the white service clubs. I couldn't believe it.'

'It was rotten, of course – but the army was following army protocol,' Neil reminded.

'It shouldn't have happened to those girls,' Laurie shot back, and Neil felt as though he'd somehow betrayed her by not echoing her rage.

'You're right,' he agreed. 'They put their lives on the line for their country, just as the white WACs did.'

'But a colored WAC I met on the ship coming home told me that in England and France they were treated like queens.'

'In our lifetime, Laurie, we're going to see awesome changes,' Neil predicted.

'That's what my brother says. Ever since the House Un-American Activities Committee was set in motion, he's been steaming about how they've wrecked the lives of so many fine people. He's constantly railing because his magazine isn't protesting more.'

'Talking about things Russian—' Neil smiled persuasively. *Here's my chance.* 'I've picked up a couple of tickets to the Boris Kerensky concert. Would you like to go with me?'

She hesitated a moment. *Does she seriously think there's something going on between Doris and me?* 'Yes,' she said with a brilliant smile. 'I love Kerensky.'

Seven

Laurie checked the small chicken in the oven that would be the basic part of dinner for the next three evenings. Another fifteen minutes, she decided and headed for the living room. Close the drapes. The days were getting shorter now. It was almost dark outside already.

As she pulled the drapes closed, she saw the television screen light up in the Winston house. She saw Neil hovering before the television set before she fully closed the drapes. No wild Saturday night for him.

But there wasn't that much to do on a Saturday in Bentonville – a drive-in movie or bowling. She was startled at this involuntary assessment. Maybe that's why small-town young got married so young. *What is the matter with me? Weigh the scales – small-town living beats city living any time. I don't have to get married to survive.*

She sat on the sofa, reached for the current edition of *Collier's*. She'd reheat last night's vegetables – that would take no more than three minutes. Again, the ugly intrusion crept into her mind. *Why did I tell Neil I'd go with him to the concert? Once we're seen together, the whole school would be whispering. 'That new teacher in the school – she's going with Neil Winston!'* There'd be some resentment, her mind taunted. Particularly from Doris Lowell.

There was nothing romantic about their relationship. They enjoyed sharing their wartime experiences. Only those who'd been part of World War II would understand that. But an inner voice intruded again. Neil Winston didn't look at her the way he'd look at a male fellow soldier.

In a sudden restlessness she decided to call Tim and Iris. She'd planned to call them tomorrow. But no one responded at their apartment. Well, of course, she derided. It was Saturday night. They'd probably gone to a play or a concert or to a party at somebody's house.

What was on television tonight? No, she should finish reading *The Wall* over the weekend. Over lunch last week she'd promised to lend it to Doris.

She grunted in annoyance at herself. Why did she feel it necessary to ingratiate herself with Doris? So she sensed some covert hostility. Everybody at the school couldn't be expected to like her.

After dinner she kicked off her shoes and stretched on the sofa with *The Wall*. Deep in the drama of the novel she was startled by the latest screeching battle between the Kendricks. They'd seemed so reserved, so pleasant when she first met them. She barely saw them since she'd moved into the apartment. Nobody seemed to have much to do with them.

'I understand his mother moved here, bought the house outright with the insurance her husband carried when he died. You know how everybody knows everybody else's business in a town like this,' Sharon had explained. 'She was a quiet, church-going woman. Once in a while her son showed up for a day or two.' That was Bud Kendrick. 'When she died, he inherited the house, moved here with his wife. He does occasional handyman jobs around town. Until a year ago she worked part-time at the supermarket. He bowls once a week with a pair of crotchety old bachelors. She goes to church on Sundays but never made friends with anybody there.'

It was clearly a marriage that never should have happened, Laurie mused, flinching at an especially loud outburst.

'You're not good for anything!' Maisie Kendrick screeched. 'You let me think – all those years I wrote to you while you were in the clink – that we'd have such a fancy life once you got out. And what did you have? This shitty house!'

'What did you have before?' he yelled back. 'A deadbeat husband who did you a favor when he died. What have you done these seventeen years but bitch about how we're not rich? You complain about havin' to cook for us. You expected a cook and a butler?'

'You let me believe—' Her voice was menacing. 'You let me believe you had a real bundle stashed away—'

'So you married me for that? That's what you're sayin'! So my partners beat me to it. That ain't my fault. I'm going for a beer – and some peace and quiet. Leave the front door open – I don't know when I'll be comin' home.'

Lucky for the Kendricks the house was set on a fairly large plot, Laurie thought. Neighbors couldn't hear the almost nightly battles. Now Laurie assessed what she'd heard. Bud Kendrick had been in prison – probably for some hefty robbery, she gathered. Maisie Kendrick had written to him while he was away – expecting him to recover the robbery heist. They were two bitter, angry people, caught in a trap of their own making.

If she'd been stupid enough to marry Phil, they would have ended up yelling at each other like that. Breaking up with Phil had saved her a lifetime of grief. Why hadn't Neil married? she wondered, was instantly self-conscious at such a thought. Probably, like herself, he saw the advantages of an uncomplicated single way of life.

On Sunday morning Laurie walked to Main Street to pick up the Sunday papers. She returned to find Neil camped on her doorstep.

'I figured you'd gone into town for the papers.' He pulled himself to his feet. 'Mom sent me over to invite you to dinner tonight. She's into her impromptu dinner party mode. She read some recipe in a new cookbook she brought home from the shop, and she can't survive without trying it out. Just three other people and you are invited. This couple she went through high school with and the fellow who runs the book shop where she works. Mom's not happy without guinea pigs to give her a verdict. I'll vouch for her – she's a great cook.'

'Sounds like fun.' *I'm doing it again – but his mother will be hurt if I reject another invitation.* 'I would have been sitting down to last night's leftovers.' *That sounds casual, doesn't it?* 'What time?'

'We're early diners. We'll sit down around seven. Pop over around six thirty? Mom always has some little surprise before dinner. I told her – she should be head chef in some fancy restaurant. But she'd read about a chef's life. Turned it down flat.'

83

'I'll be there,' Laurie promised, conscious of an odd excitement. *Why am I reacting this way?*

'That first year home after the war – I gained fifteen pounds. Mom wanted to make up for the years of Spam and C-rations.'

That's why he hasn't got married – it's so comfortable at home.

'I drowned myself in really good coffee,' Laurie recalled. 'Remember the bilge that passed for coffee in the army?'

'Remember the weird substitutes when we ran out of coffee?' He groaned in recall.

They were two World War II veterans drawn to each other because of the war, she told herself. He wasn't seeing her as an unattached girl. 'Can I bring something?'

'Just yourself.' All at once he seemed ill at ease. 'See you later.'

Laurie went into her apartment, settled down to read the *Enquirer* and the *Record*. She made a habit of reading both, though much of what she read in the *Record* was either inane or contrary to her own views. Still, she was determined to gain a real insight into the workings of the town. This was where she meant to spend the rest of her life. Later she'd wallow in the *New York Times*.

Right away, focusing on the front page of the *Record*, she felt a surge of hostility. What

84

was this garbage about 'local displeasure' at the selection of the Arts League Committee? Why must the committee limit itself to hiring only American artists? At least, the *Record* was delicate about it, she conceded. They didn't come right out and accuse Boris Kerensky of being a Communist. They stressed that he was Russian – and thereby suspect. But people would get the message. Had she been naive to expect this not to happen in a small town?

It would blow over, she told herself with determined optimism. People here were concerned about more personal things. Would the school spending deal go through? Would property taxes fly up to the sky? They'd still be a lot lower than taxes in Westchester County, where Tim and Iris were moving.

Preparing lunch for herself, Laurie found her mind traveling on a disturbing path. Almost since the first days of class she'd been bothered by – what was it, an attitude of her students? They were polite – except for the class bully. They were attentive. But she wasn't reaching them. There was a wall between them and her.

She wasn't imagining this, she told herself with frustration. It was almost as though they were afraid of her. Call Karen, she ordered herself. Discuss this with her. Not Pat or Sharon – they had a way of accepting classroom situations. She hurried through lunch – impatient to talk with Karen.

With the dishes in the sink she sat down to phone Karen. Would Karen be annoyed at being disturbed over the weekend? No, she brushed this aside.

'Hello?' Karen's voice was warm.

'Karen, do you mind calls on weekends?' she asked, all at once self-conscious. 'I mean, I have a problem—'

'Of course I don't mind,' Karen chided good-humoredly. 'And what's the problem?'

As succinctly as she could manage, Laurie explained her concern about her relationship with her class.

'I don't know what it is,' she wound up, 'but I'm not getting through to them. I'm not even sure they're learning the way they should. And I don't know how to cope with this.'

Karen exuded a heavy sigh. 'I should have put you on warning.'

'About what?' Laurie was bewildered.

'Your class was Anita Collins' second grade last year,' Karen began. 'Most of the elementary teachers knew her kids were having a bad time. She was having a real bad time with her husband, and she brought her anger to class. It got worse through the course of the school year. A couple of mothers complained. She should have been removed from the classroom, but her father

86

heads the Bentonville Bank. The bank holds a lot of mortgages. Nobody – especially not Carl Franklin – was about to antagonize him by removing Anita from teaching.'

'But that's outrageous!' Laurie was indignant.

'I know that, and you know that. And most of the teachers know it. Luckily she had a kind of breakdown early in August and went on sabbatical. But I guess her class is suffering from that school year with her.'

'Okay, I have to make them trust me,' Laurie plotted, her mind in high gear. 'I should change the environment, redesign our classroom. Instead of having their desks in a line-up, I'll put them in a circle with mine in the middle. No,' she rejected this before Karen could comment. 'I need a casual atmosphere, no constraints. I don't suppose I could get the funds to buy four small, round tables, with chairs to surround them—' Could she afford to spend the money herself?

'There're tables and chairs in the storage area,' Karen recalled. 'They were bought when it appeared we'd have an additional kindergarten class – but that fell through.'

'Should I ask Mr Franklin for permission to use them?' She couldn't afford to antagonize the principal this early in her tenure.

'Don't ask Franklin,' Karen said quickly. 'Talk to Beverly. The woman janitor,' she reminded because for the moment the name didn't register. 'Beverly has the keys to the storage area. The three of us can set up your room after school tomorrow. Franklin doesn't even have to know about it.'

'He might be furious,' Laurie began, then changed attitude. 'As long as it doesn't disturb him, he won't give a damn,' she surmised. 'Karen, let's do it!'

Late in the afternoon Laurie debated about what to wear for dinner. Instinct told her the Winstons – Neil and his mother – would be informal. Nothing 'New Look', she decided and settled on a turquoise shirtwaist that Iris said did wonderful things for her eyes. She wasn't trying to make herself attractive for Neil, she told herself defensively. It was natural to want to look her best at her first party in town.

She was dressed forty minutes before it was time to leave. She didn't want to be the first to arrive, she told herself, and waited until she saw an unfamiliar car swing into the Winstons' driveway. She watched while a tall, rangy man with unfashionably long hair walked up to the door of the Winston house. All right, go over now.

She rang the bell. Neil opened the door.

'Hi.' He wore a sports shirt – informal was the style for the night. 'I hope you're hungry. Mom's been cooking up a storm all day.' He guided her into the foyer, back towards the kitchen. 'She's still at it.'

'You're Laurie,' Beth Winston said without preliminaries. 'I hear your kids are happy with their new third grade teacher.'

'Thank you.' Laurie was startled. So quickly word circulated?

'I hope you're an adventurous eater.' A twinkle in Beth Winston's eyes. 'Sometimes I wander far afield.'

'I grew up in a variety of countries,' Laurie reassured her. 'And meals offered a lot of surprises.'

'Taste this,' Beth urged, scooping up a spoonful of soup and handing it to Laurie. 'I hope you like curry.' All at once she was anxious.

'We spent a year in New Delhi when I was eleven. I love curry – in mild portions.' She was making snap decisions again – she liked Neil's mother. She sipped the soup. 'Oh, it's wonderful!'

Neil guided her out of the kitchen now, down the hall and to the living room. The man she had seen earlier was listening to a newscaster on television, switched it off at the sight of Neil and Laurie.

'Eric, watch the news if you like,' Neil said, then introduced him to Laurie. But the TV remained off.

'Neil told me you used to live in New York.' He seemed almost worshipful.

89

'Didn't you like it?'

'It's noisy and crowded and unfriendly,' Laurie said with brutal frankness. Wasn't that how New York seemed to small-towners? What was the old cliché? 'It's a nice place to visit, but I wouldn't want to live there.'

'But what about all the museums, the theaters – Greenwich Village?' Eric challenged.

'I suppose it's a trade-off,' she said after a moment. 'There's a lot of richness in New York – but you pay for that with the ungodly noise, the crowded subways, the shoving crowds.'

'Hey, Eric, don't get any ideas,' Neil joshed. 'How would this town survive without you and the book store? Who would be here to fight for our side when the would-be local censors try to ban a book?'

Laurie was shocked. 'That happens *here*?'

'At intervals people get up on their high horse and say, "No, you can't sell that book in this town." It doesn't reach that stage very often – but Mom tells me that in his time, Eric, your father fought for freedom of thought here.'

'I was proud of him for that. Even in those last two years – when he was dying – he wrote letters to the newspapers. The *Enquirer* always ran them. The *Record* never did. And if there was a move to ban a book,

90

he made sure the book store window was loaded with copies.'

The doorbell rang. Neil went off to respond. Alone with Laurie, Eric seemed uncomfortable.

'You were born here?' Laurie asked – trying to put him at ease.

'We go back three generations.' No pride in his smile, Laurie thought. Bitterness. And all at once she understood. Eric Hunter didn't fit into the mold most local people found acceptable.

'I've always wanted to live in a town where people have lived for generations. We traipsed around the globe when I was a child. My parents were both only children – there was no close family other than my parents, my brother, and me. No aunts or uncles or cousins.'

'I'm an only child,' Eric began then stopped because Neil was ushering the newcomers into the living room.

'Eric, did you get my book in yet?' the small, round woman in her mid-fifties demanded in convivial spirits.

Before he could reply, Neil introduced Laurie to Gail and Joe Simpson.

'Gail and Joe went all through elementary and high school with Mom,' Neil told Laurie.

'I hear you've been out talking to a lot of people about the new bill that'll raise property taxes,' Joe chided Neil. 'Plugging it. Shame on you.'

'We need more classrooms for kindergarten and first grade.' Neil was serious. 'Have you any idea how the enrollment is expanding?'

'We know what all the fellows coming home from the war were doing nights,' Joe said with a chuckle, and his wife shot him a reproachful glance. 'But why do people like Gail and me have to pay the bill?'

The heated – but good-humored – argument was interrupted by Beth's arrival in the living room with a tray of canapés.

'No local politics at dinner time,' she decreed, passing the tray from one to another.

'Ooh, this is delicious,' Gail said after the first nibble. 'And probably madly fattening.' But she seemed philosophical about this.

'Everybody to the dinner table,' Beth ordered now. 'We're having my version of chicken Kiev.' She grinned. 'I'm not making a statement.'

While Beth served the soup course, Eric brought up the subject of the Boris Kerensky concert. He was incensed by the article in the *Record*.

'Can you imagine the nerve of people complaining because Kerensky doesn't happen to be an American citizen? He's one of the finest young pianists in the world today.

We're lucky to have him come here.'

'Eric, what about my book?' Gail tried again. 'You said you'd be able to get it for me in a few days.' She ignored Eric's wrath. She wasn't comfortable talking about the concert, Laurie interpreted.

'It'll probably be in tomorrow,' Eric surmised. 'I'll give you a buzz.' He paused. 'Or Beth will. Phone calls are her department now.'

'You going to the concert, Eric?' Joe asked. 'You're one of our intellectuals.'

'I won't be going to the concerts this year.' All at once Eric seemed withdrawn. 'Though I have a record album by Kerensky, and it's great.'

'Neil and Laurie are going,' Beth said and stopped short. 'Aren't you?' she asked awkwardly, glancing from one to the other. The implication inadvertent.

'We're going,' Neil confirmed, unperturbed that the others might assume he and Laurie were 'going together'. 'I suspect there won't be an empty seat in the house.'

'But doesn't it give you a funny feeling?' Gail glanced about the table. 'I mean, people rushing to hear a Russian musician – with all that's happening in Korea? You know how people are saying Moscow promoted the invasion of South Korea to see how we'd react.'

'Not many people here in town pay much

attention to what's happening in Korea.' Laurie strived to sound casual. She'd never anticipated a discussion like this in Bentonville. But she should have realized in every town there would be a few concerned people. 'If you asked most of them to point out Korea on a map, they'd never find it.'

'Except for Americans whose sons and husbands are being shipped out,' Beth pointed out gently. 'It's as though nobody here at home realizes that American soldiers are dying in Korea.'

'Gail and I aren't much for concerts,' Joe admitted. He was unnerved, Laurie guessed, by the talk about Korea. 'Give us a good movie any time. Have any of you seen *Sunset Boulevard*? Gloria Swanson is marvelous.'

'It bothers me—' Gail ignored her husband's question, 'that with so many wonderful musicians who're Americans the Arts League Committee had to choose a Russian.'

'I wish there was some shot – like a shot against diphtheria – that would immunize Americans against this Red Scare—' Laurie paused. She sensed that Neil and his mother were nervous that she talked this way. She was relieved when Eric turned the conversation to talk about New York again.

'I was there for five months – oh, almost eighteen years ago.' Laurie noted that Neil appeared astonished. This was new to him.

But then he must have been about twelve when Eric was in New York. 'I had this tiny apartment in Greenwich village – on Jane Street,' he reminisced. 'I worked in a book store on Eighth Street. Life seemed wonder ful. There was such freedom there.' His face tensed. 'Then my father got sick, and I had to come home to take over the shop.'

'I love the book stores on Eighth Street.' Laurie felt guilty at this admission. 'When I was too broke to buy, I browsed.'

'Laurie, you must visit Eric's shop,' Beth chirped. 'He has a terrific selection.'

'And if he doesn't have it, he'll get it for you,' Gail added.

'My mother – while she was alive,' Eric said, 'sometimes got nervous when I went against some of our sterling citizens.' Contempt in his voice. 'Like when a committee tried to get me not to sell *Forever Amber*. It wasn't exactly my cup of tea, but people have a right to read what they want.' Unexpectedly he grinned, turned to Neil. 'You remember telling me to put Budd Schulberg's *Disenchanted* into the window? I sold seven copies in the next two days.' Now Laurie saw a shy satisfaction creep into his eyes. 'Some people in this town don't like me – but the store does well.'

Laurie felt a surge of compassion for Eric Hunter. The knowledge that some people in this town rejected him disturbed her. This hardly fitted her image of the warm, friendly small town.

Her mind wandered from the conversation about the dinner table. The pain she saw in Eric Hunter's eyes warned her that to deviate from the town's accepted mold was to face hostility and contempt. Eric yearned to escape to the freedom of life in Greenwich Village – notable for its 'live and let live' philosophy. Why didn't he sell the shop and go there now?

Can I fit into the accepted mold? Tim is always saying I'm so impulsive – I speak out too freely. But I won't be muzzled. I'll say what I believe. Will that make me a pariah in this town?

Eight

The day was unseasonably cool. A slanting rain hammered at the classroom windows – seeming, Laurie thought, to close off the outside world. She sat at her desk while the twenty-two eight-year-olds in her class worked on the assignment that she had just given them.

Last night's small dinner party was fun, she thought. Still, it bothered her that Gail Simpson was uncomfortable with Boris Kerensky appearing at a local concert. Did the Simpsons – and Eric Hunter – think she was 'going with' Neil? If they hadn't met that way at the A&P and she hadn't mentioned being a WAC in Italy, he never would have invited her to go to the concert with him. Would he? *I don't want people in town to think I'm involved emotionally with Neil. I'm not – it's just that we happen to share war experiences.*

'Oliver, sit back in your seat,' she called out with unfamiliar sharpness to a frequent troublemaker in the back row. 'Don't pull Sally's hair. Write your story like the others.'

She worried about Oliver. He was bright – she was convinced of that. But too often he fell asleep in class. She worried about the burn on his arm last week, about his bruised cheek this morning. Something very wrong was happening to him at home, she suspected.

She was startled when the lunch bell rang. She hadn't realized it was that late.

'All right, you'll have to finish your stories after lunch.' She gazed about the room with a warm, reassuring smile. 'Now let's line up for the march to the cafeteria.'

With her students in care of the cafeteria matron Laurie chose her lunch and carried her tray down the hall to the elementary teachers' lunchroom. As usual she joined Karen, Pat, and Sharon at a corner table.

'What a depressing day,' Pat greeted her. 'If I stay awake till three o'clock, it'll be a miracle.'

'The farmers need the rain,' Sharon said. 'It was a long, hot, dry summer.'

'I'd like to be having lunch in some cozy restaurant with an open fireplace,' Karen mused.

'You're a romantic at heart.' Sharon shook her head. 'In this world it's smarter to be a realist.'

'I'm trying to be realistic about one of my kids.' Laurie was somber. 'I know something's wrong in his home.'

'You mean Daddy drinks too much and beats the hell out of Mommy?' Karen sighed. 'I ran into that last year.'

'What did you do?' Laurie asked.

'I reported it to the guidance counselor.' Karen shook her head. 'Nothing happened. In the middle of the term the family moved away.'

'This little boy had a burned arm last week. He gave me some phony explanation. This morning he had a huge bruise on his face. Why do these kids think they have to protect their parents?'

'You're better off if you just overlook it,' Sharon said. 'Franklin will tell you plainly, "We don't interfere in students' private lives."'

'But that's wrong!' Laurie began, then paused because Doris Lowell was approaching their table.

'Hi.' Doris waved airily to all four women, then focused on Laurie. 'Did you by chance remember to bring in your copy of *The Wall*?' A veiled hostility in her voice.

'Yes, I did.' *Why do I react so defensively at every encounter with Doris?* It was Doris's arrogance, Laurie decided. Her air that she was slumming by talking to other teachers. 'Stop by my room after school and pick it up.'

'I'll do that.' Doris moved on to another table.

'Did you register to vote yet?' Karen asked Laurie.

'I don't think I've lived here long enough.' Laurie was doubtful.

'You will l ave by election time. Be sure to register before then.'

'Oh, I will.' Laurie remembered Neil's eloquence over dinner when the subject arose at several intervals. Of course, she conceded, Gail and Joe Simpson's children were grown – they weren't using the school system – but couldn't they understand the importance of support for education?

'Oh God, you political-minded women,' Pat drawled. 'But I suppose some women have to go out and vote.'

'We fought a lot of years for the right.' Karen was struggling to disguise her annoyance. 'Why not take advantage?'

'You have the little Mitchell girl in your class, don't you?' Sharon asked Laurie. To change the topic, Laurie interpreted. Sharon probably voted – but following her father's instructions.

'Betsy Mitchell.' Laurie's smile was warm. 'Such a darling little girl.'

'Did you ever see a child who looked like such a fashion plate?' Sharon sighed. 'Poor little kid. I had her in the first grade. At a class Halloween party she dropped a chunk of chocolate ice-cream on her dress and cried. I gather her mother would have been so-o upset.' Scorn deepened Sharon's voice. 'I managed to wash away the stain and all was saved.'

'Sally Mitchell's got political ambitions. For her husband,' Pat added. 'Sally gets herself on just about every committee in town. I suppose she thinks it's making contacts for him. He's an insurance salesman. My oldest sister went to high school with him – she says he'd talked about being a lawyer, but who had money for college in the Depression? Then once Sally decided Donald just might have a future selling insurance, she went after him. She had Betsy seven months after the honeymoon.'

'Pat, you know every bit of gossip in this town,' Sharon clucked.

Pat giggled. 'My father calls me Mrs Winchell.'

It was raining heavily when Laurie dismissed her class for the day. Were they dressed warmly enough, she fretted – then noticed that Betsy Mitchell was shyly approaching her.

'Yes, Betsy?' Laurie smiled encouragingly.

'Miss Evans, my mother told me to wait for her in our room if it was raining. She'll be taking me to my piano lesson. She oughta be here now.' All at once Betsy was anxious.

'I'll wait here with you,' Laurie soothed.

101

'Something probably held her up for a few minutes.'

Betsy's winsome face lighted. 'I'm glad you're my teacher, Miss Evans. You're awful nice – and real pretty, too.'

'Thank you, Betsy. I'm very fond of you, too. I'm glad you're in my class.'

'Hi.' Doris strolled into the classroom. 'You said you'd brought in your copy of *The Wall*—'

'Right, Doris.' Laurie reached into a desk drawer for the book.

'Oh, have you heard?' Doris's smile was oddly triumphant. 'The word just came through. Boris Kerensky's concert is being canceled.'

'Oh, I'm disappointed!' Laurie sighed. 'I'd been so looking forward to it. Did he have an accident?'

'An accident that he was unmasked. The man's a suspected Commie. The committee wired the New York booking office and canceled as soon as they realized this.'

'You said "suspected",' Laurie pinpointed. 'What proof do they have?'

'Mrs Gaines just came back from visiting her daughter over in Linwood – and she told the committee the Kerensky concert had been canceled there because of the ugly stories. Of course, there'll be ticket refunds.'

'But what proof do they have that he's a Communist?' Laurie challenged. 'How can they cancel a concert at the last moment this way because of rumors?'

'Oh, it's more than just rumors.' Doris brushed this aside. 'The committee over at Linwood was told that he'd appeared at benefits for the Loyalists in Spain – you know, the Communists who fought against Franco.'

'That doesn't mean he's a Communist.' Tim had fought in the Abraham Lincoln Brigade. He'd come home so disillusioned about the Spanish Civil War. *'Damn, Laurie – it was Communism versus Fascism. Only the blind – like me – believed it was a fight for democracy.'*

'He signed petitions – oh, all sorts of things. It was in some magazine – the whole rotten story!'

'What magazine?' Laurie challenged. Working in television, Iris knew about *Red Channels* and the horror it was creating. But the average person didn't know about it. 'What magazine?' Laurie pressed.

'I don't know exactly.' Doris was impatient. 'But it was there in print. The committee can't sponsor a man like that.'

'The committee doesn't actually know anything. It's all just hearsay, isn't it?' Laurie struggled for calm.

'Oh, come on, Laurie. Don't be naive. He can't be entirely innocent. Where there's smoke there's bound to be fire. We're living in dangerous times.'

'Oh, I agree with you.' Laurie's eyes blazed. 'Dangerous to our freedom when a rumor is accepted as truth! Don't you realize that you or I or anybody else can be branded a Communist because somebody feels like saying it?'

Doris stared at Laurie – as though she had uttered some gross obscenity, Laurie thought. 'We have to protect the decent people in this country against the bad elements.'

'I think it's horrible to cancel the concert on the strength of some unsubstantiated rumor.' *How can this be happening in a small town like Bentonville? I thought it was confined to Hollywood and New York and Washington.* 'I'd be ashamed to be a member of that committee.'

'I wouldn't repeat that around.' Doris gazed out the window for a moment. 'Wouldn't you know I'd have a dental appointment on a miserable day like this?'

'Betsy?' A jewelry-laden blonde in a wasp-waisted dress hovered in the doorway. 'Oh, hello, Doris.' Both women seemed wary at this encounter, Laurie thought in a corner of her mind as Doris returned the greeting and sailed past. Somewhere along the line, she surmised, they'd clashed.

'Mommy—' Betsy leaped to her feet. 'You're late.' A faint hint of reproach in her voice.

'I'm sorry, sweetie.' Sally Mitchell contrived a smile as she turned to Laurie. 'I gather you're Miss Evans, Betsy's teacher?'

'Yes. Betsy is delightful. It's a pleasure to have her in my class.' Laurie's words brought a dazzling smile to Betsy's small face.

'I hope I haven't held you up?' Sally Mitchell gestured to Betsy to sit down so she could pull on bright red boots.

'Not at all.' Laurie remembered what Pat had said at lunch about Sally Mitchell being the perpetual committee woman. But she suspected that to Sally Mitchell teachers were low on the totem pole.

'We'd better dash. I don't want to be late for Betsy's piano lesson.' With a perfunctory smile for Laurie, Sally Mitchell prodded Betsy towards the door.

Sally Mitchell held an opened umbrella over Betsy and herself while they hurried to her car in the parking area.

'Today just got out of hand,' Sally complained when she and Betsy were settled in the car. 'I wanted to have time to fix your hair before your lesson.'

Betsy giggled. 'I don't play the piano with my hair.'

'But I like the picture of you sitting at the piano and looking so pretty.' She paused for a few moments, focused on backing out of the parking area. 'What was Doris Lowell doing in your classroom?' She'd loathed Doris since their senior year in high school, when Doris had gone to their senior prom with the boy she had been pursuing.

'She was talking with Miss Evans about some concert.' Betsy squinted in recall.

'What did she say?' Sally was all at once alert.

'Miss Lowell said the concert had been canceled. And then—' Betsy paused.

'Then what?'

'Then Miss Evans said she thought it was—' Betsy searched her mind. 'She said she thought it was horrible.'

'Oh, did she!' Sally bristled. Her anger transferred to Laurie now. 'What else did she say?' The School Board never should have hired an out-of-towner. The job should have gone to Emily Pierce. So Emily did quit two teaching posts in the past five years – she probably had good reasons. 'Betsy?' she prodded. 'What else did Miss Evans say?'

'She said she'd be ashamed to be on the committee. Gee, she's pretty when she gets mad. Her eyes get all sparkly.'

'How dare she! I'm on that committee!'

'Mommy, what's a Communist?'

'A very bad person, Betsy. And from the way she talks, Miss Evans is one of them.'

'No.' Betsy was adamant. 'She's real nice. I like her.'

'I'm not sure I want you to remain in her class. Not a woman who stands up for a Communist.'

'I want to stay in her class, Mommy, I like her! I like her!' Betsy began to cry.

'She said nasty things about your mother.' Sally's face was thunderous. 'I'm on that committee.'

Laurie Evans isn't going around town maligning my committee. She's asking for trouble – and she's going to get it!

Nine

On arrival at school this morning Laurie had talked with Beverly about rearranging her classroom. Beverly had been delighted to be helpful. Now at the end of the day – with the school devoid of students and teachers – Laurie and Karen worked with Beverly to remove the traditional desks, replacing them with four round tables and small chairs that gave the room an aura of playtime. Laurie's desk occupied a spot in the circle formed by the tables. Karen had brought a collection of colorful prints to hang about the walls.

'Oh, I like it.' Her eyes roaming about the room, Laurie glowed. 'I think the kids will respond to this kind of informality. Karen, thanks so much!' Tomorrow she'd bring in a small gift for Beverly.

'It's the creative touch the kids need after a year with Madam Horror.' Karen smiled in satisfaction. 'But I'd better run. I promised to give Howie a hand at the office this afternoon.'

Laurie loaded her tote, collected her

umbrella, prepared to leave for the day. She ought to go over to the office and talk to Mr Franklin about Oliver. No doubt in her mind that the poor little kid was being abused at home. Still, she dreaded the encounter. She remembered what Sharon had said when she'd talked about Oliver at lunch today: *'You're better off if you just overlook it. Franklin will tell you plainly. "We don't interfere in students' private lives."'* But how could she stand by and do nothing?

At the office Laurie asked to see the principal.

'This will take just a few minutes,' she cajoled.

'Oh, he's gone for the day,' the school secretary told her. 'You can see him before classes start tomorrow morning. He's always available by eight a.m.'

'I'll be here,' Laurie promised.

She left the office with a growing sense of frustration – upset about Oliver and fearing an impasse when she spoke to Mr Franklin in the morning, upset about Doris's reaction to the cancellation of the concert. Would others in town agree with Doris that it was the right thing to do? She couldn't believe that.

Involuntarily she thought about Neil. He'd be upset, she decided with a sense of vindication. Wouldn't he? Suddenly it was urgent to discuss this with him. How could something like this happen in a pleasant little town like Bentonville? It happened in large cities where major newspapers loudly took one side or the other.

Was Neil still at school? She'd driven to school this morning because of the rain. Neil had probably walked – so he could leave the car for his mother. She made a hasty survey of the cars in the parking area. No sign of his gray Chevy. Maybe he was still here. She hurried down the corridor that led to the high school classrooms. Neil was striding towards her.

'Would you like a lift home?' She tried to sound casual. 'The rain's coming down heavy again.'

'I'd love it.' He grinned. 'I shower in the morning – that's enough for one day.'

'I stopped by the office hoping to talk to Franklin.' She fell into step beside Neil – heading back towards the school entrance. Once they were in the car, she'd ask him if he'd heard about the concert. 'Of course, he's out of here as fast as the students.'

'Problems?' Neil asked with a compassionate smile.

While they left the school and hurried – under the protection of Laurie's umbrella – to her car, Laurie explained her fears about Oliver. Neil listened, his face somber.

Neil sighed. 'It's a bad situation. I had a case like that two years ago. A fourteen-

year-old who was obviously being abused –
but every time I tried to question him, he
was evasive. These kids don't want to admit
their bad home situations.'

'What did Franklin do about it?'

'I didn't even bother taking it to him,' Neil
said after a moment. 'I knew he'd brush the
whole thing under the rug. I went straight to
the parents, talked to them.'

'Did it work?'

'Not the way I'd hoped.' Neil's face con-
veyed his frustration. 'The father broke the
kid's arm. The emergency room called in
the cops. The kid refused to implicate his
father. The police had to let him go. The
father walked out on the family three weeks
later.'

'And the guidance counselor was useless,'
Laurie surmised.

'The guidance counselor doesn't get
involved beyond matters that involve school
work,' Neil said flatly. 'That's how the job is
set up. ' He reached for the umbrella, held it
for Laurie while she climbed behind the
wheel of the car.

Not until she'd driven away from the
school did Laurie bring up the subject of
the Kerensky concert.

'I suppose you've heard about the concert?'

'What about it?'

'It's been canceled.'

111

'By whom? Why? Is Kerensky ill?'

'The concert committee canceled it because some woman named Gaines came back from Linwood to report that it had been canceled there. The Red Scare deal.' Laurie grimaced. 'Right away, Doris said, the committee called the New York booking office and canceled the concert here.'

'That's absurd!' Neil's voice was scathing. 'They shouldn't have jumped to conclusions because of what happened in Linwood!'

'I blame part of this on that article in the *Record*.'

'I don't read the *Record*,' Neil said.

'Oh, they hinted that Kerensky is Russian – and therefore suspect.' Laurie's mind leaped into high gear. 'I'm going to write a letter to the editorial page of the *Enquirer*. What's the name of the editor?'

'Jim Peters,' Neil told her, then hesitated. 'It might be better to wait and see if this gets reversed.'

'You expect the committee to change their minds?' Why is Neil all at once backtracking? A minute ago he was as furious as I am. 'That's not going to happen, Neil.'

'Give them a chance to reconsider before you shoot a letter off to the *Enquirer*.' He seemed to be searching for words. 'You're new at the school. Sometimes it's wise to tread lightly when you're in a public job like teaching.'

'Why should we be afraid to say what we believe? We're not living behind the Iron Curtain.'

'This is a small town,' Neil began. 'We—'

'Because it's a small town I think we should speak out. Every voice is important. You know how awful it is when unsubstantiated rumors are regarded as facts. Just because a neighboring town does something stupid we don't have to follow suit. Somebody has to make that committee realize what a terrible mistake they're making.'

'Wait a few days, Laurie. You're new in town. Let somebody else go to bat on this.'

'I know about the feuds over the new playground and the recreation center and all.' Laurie had heard Karen argue about the need for these in town – and she and Howie, Karen pointed out, were fighting for them. 'But this is a strike against democracy!'

'You don't know small towns the way I do.' Neil was troubled. 'You go after that committee, and they'll make life miserable for you.'

'I'm not going after anybody. I just think that people ought to know what's going on – so they can put a stop to it. We live in a democracy, Neil. Let's act like it.'

'Wait a few days,' he coaxed. 'Then if you still feel it's important, write to the *Enquirer*.'

113

'All right.' *Tim always complains that I'm too impulsive – too quick on the draw.* 'I'll wait a few days. But I don't expect the situation to change.' A hint of defiance in her voice.

'What about coming to the house for dinner tonight?' he invited. 'You and Mom can get hot under the collar together.'

'You can't just invite me to dinner without discussing it with your Mom first,' she scolded.

'Mom always cooks enough for a boarding house. I told her – she missed her vocation. She'd have been happy running a restaurant – with a lot of people to feed. And she likes you. In Mom's eyes you're very special.' And his own eyes said he felt the same way.

'If you're sure,' she wavered. Preparing a lonely dinner seemed suddenly uninviting.

It isn't that I'm getting emotionally involved with Neil. It's that Neil and his mother and I are so simpatico.

Ten

Sally Mitchell sat in her usual club chair in the room of the miniature Victorian that Betsy's music teacher referred to as 'my studio'. On most occasions she enjoyed sitting in on Betsy's lessons, though she knew that Miss Johnson privately resented her presence. But today she was impatient for the lesson to be over. She had phone calls to make. She seethed at what she considered an outrageous reaction to her civic duty.

'Very good, Betsy,' Miss Johnson approved. 'Now make sure you practice your scales for half an hour each day.'

'Oh, she will.' Sally rose to her feet, reached into her purse for cash. Miss Johnson preferred that to a check. 'We'll see you next week at the same time.' For an instant she considered discussing the cancellation of the concert, discarded this. She wanted to make those phone calls.

At home Sally settled Betsy with milk and a cookie at her record player to listen to *Peter and the Wolf*, then hurried to the phone

115

to call her husband.

'Mitchell Insurance,' the voice of his secretary came over the line.

'Claire, may I speak to my husband, please?'

'Sure, Sally. Just a minute.'

'Hi, Sally.' Donald's voice was guarded.

Why does he always think when I call him at the office there's a problem?

'What's up?'

'Have you got a couple of minutes?' she asked. 'This is important,' she emphasized because he liked to keep personal calls brief during office hours.

'Sure.'

'You know about the concert the end of next week?' He'd go but he'd be bored to death.

'Yeah?'

'Well, it's been canceled. Boris Kerensky's been accused of Commie affiliations, so naturally we called the booking office and insisted that Bentonville be eliminated from his tour. But that arrogant little slut who's Betsy's teacher – I hear she's chasing madly after Neil Winston – had the nerve to call us terrible for taking the action it was our duty to take. She said this right in Betsy's presence!' Her voice grew shrill. 'In front of a young, impressionable child!'

'I doubt that Betsy understood.' Her husband shrugged this off.

'Donald, do you honestly think this is the kind of woman who should be teaching our child?'

'Sally, don't get hysterical over this.' Irritation crept into his voice.

'I don't know why they couldn't have hired Emily Pierce. I haven't liked Laurie Evans since the moment I set eyes on her.'

'They didn't hire Emily because she's an irresponsible little twit,' Donald pointed out. 'Sally, I have to make some calls—'

'We'll talk about this later. You will be home at a reasonable time?'

'I'll be in the house by six,' he said tiredly. 'You won't have to hold up dinner.'

Sally sat before the phone in contemplation. Call Alice Brenner, she decided. As a member of the concert committee, she'd want to know what was happening. She gave the operator Alice's number, waited impatiently for someone to pickup. They couldn't just sit back and do nothing!

'Hello?'

'Alice, it's me,' Sally began, her voice already climbing upward. 'The word's racing around town already about the cancellation. I—'

'You expected that, didn't you? People will be sorry to miss the concert. But they'll understand it was our duty as committee members to cancel.'

'Wait till you hear what Laurie Evans said.

117

You won't believe it!'

'Who's Laurie Evans?'

'The new third grade teacher. The one who's chasing after Neil Winston. It looks like local girls aren't good enough for him,' she pointed out aggrievedly. 'Anyhow, let me tell you what happened.'

In elaborate detail Sally reported what Betsy had told her.

'I called Donald right away and told him, but you know men. He accused me of making a mountain out of a molehill – because Betsy's always talking about how wonderful her teacher is.'

'How did she manage to hook Neil? Doris has been after him since he came home from the army.'

'She lives right across the way – in the apartment in that awful Kendrick house. From the moment she landed in town, she's poked her nose into everything. As though she'd lived here all her life. But how dare she talk that way about the concert committee!'Sally's voice soared in fresh rage. 'When we work so hard to bring a little culture into town.'

'I think we deserve a lot of credit. It isn't easy to get important artists to a town this size.'

'Such nerve, Alice – to go out of her way like that to defend some Communist.'

'Well, you know what they say – birds of a

feather—'

A surge of triumph shot through Sally. 'You think that, too.'

'Why else would she be so furious?' Alice demanded.

'That's been in the back of my mind ever since it happened,' Sally admitted. 'But I wanted to hear you say it first. You know I always lean over backwards before condemning anyone.'

'How obvious do you expect her to be?' Alice drawled. 'She's not going to show you her Communist Party card.'

'I'd be the last one in town to start something – but I do think people should know what's going on.'

'You should take this right to Mr Franklin, Sally. Let him see what's going on right under his eyes.' The atmosphere was suddenly electric. 'Thank God, neither of my two are in her class – but she's got twenty-two trusting little souls in the palms of her hands.'

'Go with me to see Mr Franklin in the morning,' Sally pounced.

'Let's wait a bit.' Alice backtracked. 'Bill gets so upset when I get involved in anything like this. Let's talk about it in a day or so – when we've both cooled down.'

Laurie glanced at the clock. Almost time to go over to Neil's house. The rain had stopped. No need for boots and an umbrella. But she was self-conscious about accepting Neil's invitation. He should have talked to his mother first. She felt like an intruder, going over for dinner on such short notice this way.

There was a definite chill in the air – a little heat would be nice. She touched the radiator. Nothing coming up. But then the Kendricks were always arguing about the cost of everything. They'd probably wait until the house was an iceberg before sending up heat. She might have to invest in an electric heater when the temperature dropped into low numbers.

She checked her watch. It was time to leave. Mrs Winston – Beth, she corrected herself because Neil's mother liked being called by her given name – wouldn't be annoyed she was coming to dinner in slacks, would she? No, Beth was an informal dresser. She reached for a jacket, hurried out into the early evening.

Neil opened the door in answer to her ring. Tempting aromas drifted from the kitchen.

'Mom's cooking up a storm. You'd better be hungry.'

'I'm starving,' Laurie said, relishing the warmth that seemed to permeate this house. 'And you have heat coming up.' Her smile was blissful.

'The temperature took a nosedive. Mom likes the house to be comfortable.' He strolled with Laurie into the living room where a television newscaster was reporting on the day's activities in Korea.

General MacArthur had announced that Seoul had fallen. Nehru voiced the fear that the invasion of North Korea could trigger the entry of China and even Russia into what was still being referred to as a 'police action'.

'Neil, turn off the news!' his mother called from the kitchen. 'I want us to enjoy dinner.'

'You told her about the concert?' Laurie sat on the comfortable but time-worn sofa.

'She'd heard already – and she's furious,' Neil said beside Laurie. 'But we're in the minority.'

'I thought all the trouble was in Hollywood and in New York. I didn't expect the craziness to reach out to average American towns.'

'I hope you're hungry.' Beth Winston walked into the dining room with a platter of succulent beef. The table was already set. 'I made a lot. Come to the table.'

'Mom, you always make a lot,' Neil joshed. 'I think you have a devious motive. This way you won't have to cook tomorrow evening – just heat.'

'Laurie, try the boeuf bourguignon. It's straight out of the new edition of *Joy of*

121

Cooking. Neil calls it my "drunken pot roast". Let me know if I overdid the wine.'

'It looks heavenly.' Laurie helped herself to a generous portion.

'I'll bring in the vegetables and salad.' Beth hurried into the kitchen.

'It's a good thing I walk a lot,' Neil mused. 'Or I'd have a real obesity problem.'

Beth returned with bowls precariously crowded on a tray. Neil rushed to help.

'The beef is magnificent.' Laurie ate with relish. 'Just the right amount of wine.'

'Laurie, you must be fuming.' Beth sat at the table. 'This business about the concert—'

'I'm fuming,' Laurie confirmed.

'I heard about it this afternoon.' Beth shook her head in distaste. 'Eric returned from an errand, and he was steaming. The nerve of that ridiculous committee!'

'It got around town fast.' Laurie's smile was eloquent.

'Honey, nothing stays secret here for more than a few minutes.' Beth chuckled. 'It's probably in this evening's *Record* – though, of course, we don't read that rag.'

'I told Neil I want to write a letter to the editor of the *Enquirer*—' Laurie paused, startled by the expression on Beth's face. 'Neil said I should hold up for a while—' Her voice trailed off.

'You're in a delicate position,' Beth said

122

gently. 'I mean, a new teacher in our school system. You could be stepping on a lot of toes.'

'But how can we not be furious?' Laurie gazed at Beth in astonishment. She'd expected major support from Neil and his mother.

'Sit back for a few days and see how the town reacts,' Beth urged after a swift glance in Neil's direction. 'Wait to see if somebody who's lived here for years fights the committee's decision. It'll have a lot more weight than a complaint from you. To the town you're a newcomer with no clout.'

'My brother Tim would say that.' Laurie considered this for a moment. 'But who'll be next? It's as though this town has set up its own House Un-American Activities Committee – and is behaving just as badly.'

'Eric agrees with you.' For a moment Beth seemed ambivalent. 'But we have to live with the people in this town. We need to tread with care.'

'The *Enquirer* might not run your letter,' Neil warned. 'After all, a newspaper depends on its advertisers for survival. And we know that the *Enquirer* is usually just a few steps ahead of the sheriff.'

'I had such a different vision of what living in a small town would be like,' Laurie said passionately.

'Everything in life comes with a price tag.

There's much that's fine in this town – but sometimes we have to look the other way, no matter how furious we are. Oh, by the way,' Beth diverted the conversation, 'Eric thinks you're just wonderful.'

'Me?' For a moment Laurie was startled. 'Oh, you mean because I lived in New York.'

'He's had such a rough life.' Beth's voice deepened with compassion. 'He was so happy those few months he lived in New York, and then he had to come home to take over running the store. And when his father died six years later, he discovered his mother was going into senility. He was so good with her – all the years she had left. No mother could have wanted a better son.'

'Why didn't he sell the shop when his mother died and go back to New York?' Laurie asked. 'What's kept him here?'

'I think he's afraid to leave now,' Neil picked up. 'It probably would have been the best thing in the world for him if he'd been drafted – he was still in his early thirties when this country went into the war, but he was rejected for service.'

'Another strike against him in the eyes of local people,' Beth recalled. 'But then they looked askance at any able-bodied man who wasn't in uniform.'

'But why stay in a place where he's so unhappy?' Laurie burst out.

'At nineteen he could be impulsive,' Beth

said. 'At forty-one he's wary. He knows what he has here. He doesn't know what he'll find in a strange city.'

A burst of thunder crackled in the night skies, shattered the quiet.

'I thought the rain was over.' Beth glanced towards the window. 'This could finish off my roses.'

Now rain began to hit the side of the house. Neil leaped to his feet. 'I'd better close the window I left open in my bedroom.'

'My son the fresh air fiend,' Beth jibed.

'It was a wonderful dinner,' Laurie thanked Beth with warmth as she prepared to leave. 'Everything was so good.'

'I'll get an umbrella and walk you home,' Neil said. 'If this keeps up all night, we'll need rowboats in the morning.'

With a steady downpour pelting the earth, Neil and Laurie ran across to her apartment. At the door he took the key from her, unlocked the door.

'Laurie, could I come in for a couple of minutes? We need to talk—'

'We've talked a lot,' she said with a light laugh, but she pushed the door wide in obvious agreement. Her heart was pounding. *What does he want to talk about?*

'I keep feeling you're running away from me,' he said when he'd closed the door behind them.

'That's crazy, Neil.' Avoiding his eyes, she reached for the umbrella, crossed with it to the kitchen.

'From the moment I saw you I knew I wanted you to be a part of my life forever.'

'When you thought I was breaking and entering?' she joshed.

'Even then.' He tried to match her effort at lightness as he reached for her hand. 'I think I always knew it would happen this way. Somebody would walk into my life, and I'd know instantly that this was the girl for me. The one for the rest of my life.'

'It wasn't supposed to happen this way.' Laurie's voice was unsteady.

'Why not?' He pulled her into his arms – his eyes searching hers.

'Because I'd convinced myself there was no room in my life for this. I like being independent. I like making my own decisions. I had a close call,' she admitted. *But I didn't feel this way about Phil. I've never felt this way about anybody.* 'And then I realized how wrong it would have been for me.'

'We'll take it slowly,' he promised. 'No rush. But I wanted you to know how I feel. Slow and easy,' he emphasized. 'But you know.'

Eleven

The wind-driven rain pounded against the house. At one point the lights in Laurie's bedroom flickered as she prepared for bed. Were they going to lose power? she wondered in a corner of her mind. But her thoughts were dominated by what was said in those few minutes alone with Neil.

It had seemed so beautiful when he reached out to her that way, pulled her close. She closed her eyes, heard his voice – so warm, so confident: *'From the moment I saw you I knew I wanted you to be a part of my life forever.'*

But how would it be later? her mind challenged. Iris always laughed and said men were a breed apart. Tim always said that Iris could work as long as she liked – but did he mean it? Iris's words – about how men coming home from the war all wanted to see their wives staying home, taking care of the house, raising kids – were etched on her mind. She still flinched at the memory of Phil's attitude, which echoed this.

The ring of the phone was shrill in the

night quiet. She reached to pick up.

'Hello?'

'Laurie?' It was Karen.

'Right, Karen.'

'I hope I'm not calling too late. Tomorrow is a school day.'

'It's not too late,' Laurie reassured her.

'I tried to reach you earlier, but you were out. Have you heard the news about the concert?'

'Yes!' Fresh rage surged in Laurie. 'Isn't it insane?'

'Howie said he wasn't that surprised. He told me that the Arthur Miller play – *Death of a Salesman* – was scheduled to play in Peoria, but there's talk that it may be canceled. Some rabid anti-Communist told an American Legion group the play was "Communist-dominated". Of course, we're a hell of a lot smaller than Peoria,' Karen conceded.

'I was talking with Neil and his mother about my writing a letter to the *Enquirer* in protest. They figured it would be better coming from someone who's lived here a long time.'

'Howie gave me that same routine. We've just been here two years – we're outsiders.'

'But suppose nobody who's been here for four generations surfaces?' Laurie challenged. 'Are we to ignore the situation?'

'Let's play it by ear. You and I get hot

under the collar real fast. If nobody comes out, then we'll do something,' Karen promised. She hesitated. 'Howie didn't say it, but I suspect he's afraid he'll chase away prospective clients if we get too noisy about this.'

'I'll wait a few days,' Laurie agreed reluctantly. 'If nobody comes out to fight this, then I'm writing a letter to the *Enquirer*.'

'Jim Peters thinks the way we do,' Karen reminded, 'but he can't afford to drive away advertisers.'

'I'll write a letter if nothing happens in the next few days,' Laurie repeated. 'I can't sit back and say nothing when I know something horrible is happening.'

'It's late – we'd both better call it a night,' Karen said. 'See you tomorrow.'

While she ate breakfast, Laurie focused on how to approach Mr Franklin about her suspicions that Oliver was being abused at home. It was the school's responsibility to intervene in situations like this, wasn't it? Yet she remembered what Sharon had said when she'd talked about Oliver at lunch. *'You're better off if you just overlook it. Franklin will tell you plainly. "We don't interfere in students' private lives."'*

But how could the school overlook a situation like this? She felt sick – remembering the burn on his arm last week, the bruise on his face yesterday, the way he kept falling

129

asleep in class. Something was definitely wrong in his family life. Why did these poor little abused kids try to cover for a parent or parents who mistreated them?

Leaving the apartment she recalled that this was one of Neil's early mornings at school. It was startling to realize how much she missed his presence on the mornings he went in early.

Arriving at the school she saw Carl Franklin's car in the parking area. He'd be in his office. Her heart began to pound. Karen had got nowhere when she'd gone to bat for a student. Could she do better? Sharon didn't think so.

She went directly to Franklin's office. His secretary was hanging away her jacket.

'He's here. Just knock on his door,' she told Laurie.

Striving for calm, Laurie knocked.

'Come in,' he ordered briskly.

'I'll just take a few moments of your time,' Laurie said cajolingly. Franklin was noted for making such meetings brief.

'Sit down, Miss Evans.' Already he was wary.

'Thank you.'

Laurie launched into her prepared statement about Oliver. Moments later he intervened with a wave of one hand.

'Miss Evans, the job of this school is to teach. We don't interfere in family lives.' He began to shuffle papers on his desk.

'But Oliver is being mistreated,' she began passionately. 'That poor little boy is—'

'Is his parents' responsibility. I understand your feelings, but it's not our job to intervene. Now if you'll excuse me—'

Seething with frustration Laurie left his office, strode down the hall towards the elementary school wing. Did Oliver have to wait until he landed in the hospital for someone to recognize what was happening to him? Never, she thought, had she expected something like this to happen in a serene little town like Bentonville.

Laurie walked into her redesigned classroom with a blend of anticipation of her students' reaction and frustration at Carl Franklin's reaction to Oliver's plight. She wasn't giving up on finding a way to stop Oliver's abuse at home, she told herself defiantly. There must be a way.

She settled herself at her desk. Bring in some potted plants, she told herself. Let the children take turns on watering duty. She glanced up with a warm smile as the first two little girls walked into the room. Their eyes were wide with astonishment. Their smiles told her they approved. All right, she comforted herself. She was doing something right.

In line at the cafeteria at lunch time Laurie

was conscious of furtive glances in her direction. Doris had spread the word about her reaction to the concert cancellation, she surmised. She should have anticipated that. With a determined smile she left the cafeteria and walked into the elementary teachers' lunchroom. Pat and Sharon were already seated. Karen was running late today.

'Hi.' Laurie slid into her usual place at the table. 'Thank God, the sun came out today. Yesterday was so gloomy.'

'What did you do to make Sally Mitchell so mad at you?' Pat asked.

'Me?' Laurie lifted an eyebrow in astonishment. 'I saw her for a few moments yesterday. What's this all about?'

'She was talking to my married sister last night about maybe asking to have her kid transferred out of your class. I didn't have a chance to finish the conversation with my sister because her four-year-old dumped the sugar bowl all over the kitchen floor.'

Laurie was bewildered. 'Mrs Mitchell picked up Betsy in the classroom yesterday – she seemed all right then.'

'It – uh—' Sharon hesitated. 'It might have something to do with your being so angry about the concert being canceled.'

Laurie's mind moved into high gear. 'Doris,' she pinpointed. 'I was quite outspoken, and she said, "I wouldn't repeat

132

that if I were you." But she obviously repeated it.'

Sharon was uneasy. 'Denise Spencer – she's the elementary school's PTA president – called me last evening. She asked what I knew about you. I said you were a first-rate teacher, that your students love you.'

'Oh, that Doris.' Pat grimaced. 'She's such a troublemaker.'

'I still think it was a horrible thing to do – to cancel the concert because of some silly rumors.' Laurie glanced from Pat to Sharon. 'Did either of you see the *Enquirer* this morning? Was there anything in it about the concert?'

'I'm never conscious enough to read the paper in the morning.' Pat shrugged. 'Whatever's important my father is sure to tell me.'

'My folks don't subscribe to the *Enquirer*,' Sharon admitted. 'They don't like Jim Peters. Not since he campaigned for Truman.'

Laurie glanced up with a welcoming smile as Karen approached.

'You're the subject of a lot of conversations around town,' Karen reported grimly. 'The phones were buzzing last night, I gather. Three teachers asked me this morning if I'd heard that the new teacher was a Commie sympathizer.'

'Oh, God!' Pat gaped in shock. 'You don't

133

want the School Board hearing talk like that.'

'I'm writing a letter to the *Enquirer*,' Laurie said. *People should understand what craziness is moving in with hurricane force.*

Karen frowned. 'Howie would say, "Wait for an old-timer to get on a soap-box." But will that happen?'

'I'm not waiting to find out. Somebody has to make this town realize what's happening here – and the *Enquirer* can do that.'

For the rest of the school day Laurie fought to keep her mind on dealing with her class. How could a few minutes of conversation with Doris have escalated into suspicions that she was a Commie sympathizer? She was impatient for the day to be over, to go home and sit down and write a letter to Jim Peters at the *Enquirer*.

Everything she'd heard about him indicated he would be as upset about this situation as she was. And they weren't alone. Neil and his mother were disturbed. Karen and Howie. And there must be others. This lovely little town mustn't become infected with bigotry and intolerance. That wasn't the American way.

Today Laurie was relieved that the whole class trooped out at the closing bell. But they'd made it clear with exuberant comments that they were pleased with the changes in their classroom. Hands had shot up when she'd invited volunteers to water the plants she meant to bring into the room. The tension she'd felt in them – even after a summer vacation away from 'Madam Horror' – seemed to be lessening. No screaming, no temper tantrums from their new teacher, she vowed.

Nobody lingered to ask questions. She suspected there'd be much talk on their school bus about the new look in their classroom. She loaded her tote and left the classroom, headed for the lobby. Arriving there she found Neil waiting at the door,

'Hi.' His smile was warm. 'It's a great day out there. I figured we'd walk home together.'

'Great.' But she was disconcerted by what she read in his eyes. Would the others notice, too? Yet at the same time she exulted in the knowledge that his own feelings matched hers. *This isn't like with Phil. It's different.*

'Hi, Mr Winston.' A pretty teenager sidled past them, along with another teenager who lifted a hand in flip greeting.

'Hey, did you two order this gorgeous day?' he joshed.

Both girls giggled. 'Sure did,' one said with a pert smile.

Laurie was conscious of their covert inspection. The two of them had a crush on Neil, she thought indulgently.

Fighting to control their giggles Jean and Kathy hurried out the door and down the stairs.

'Isn't he cute?' Jean whispered. 'And so mature.'

'Yeah, not like the dumb boys we know.' Kathy sighed. 'Everybody knows he's nutty over that new teacher.'

'She's real pretty. Lots prettier than Miss Lowell. And younger,' Jean added with a malicious smile. 'Miss Lowell's got to be in her thirties.' She lowered her voice. 'An old maid.'

'I heard my old man talking about her last night.' Kathy frowned in recall. 'He was talking on the phone with some fella from his office – and this fella said she's really a Commie.'

'Go on—' Jean stared in disbelief.

'I heard my father tell my mother about her. She's a Commie. They sent her to infiltrate the school.'

'That's crazy.' Jean grimaced in rejection.

'I know – you expect Commie women to walk around in flat heels and have an urgent need for falsies. Remember Greta Garbo in *Ninotchka*? I mean, before they made her look so gorgeous.'

'I don't believe she's a Commie,' Jean insisted. 'People say such awful things without any proof.'

The sun provided such warmth as Laurie walked towards her house with Neil that she unbuttoned her jacket.

'This is a beautiful Indian summer,' she said ebulliently. 'Oh, I love this weather.'

'Why don't we drive out to the lake and feed the ducks?' Neil suggested with a brilliant smile. 'This is a day to be treasured.' He glanced across the road. 'Mom walked to the shop today – she didn't take the car.'

'I'll run inside and get some bread.' Her pulse was racing. It was broad daylight, she assured herself. Nothing could happen. They'd drive out to the lake and feed the ducks. But it would be so nice to be there with Neil.

They managed light conversation while they drove to the lake, but each was super-conscious of the other's presence. Laurie told herself not to talk about the letter she meant to write tonight to Jim Peters and to hand deliver tomorrow afternoon to the *Enquirer*.

At the sun-caressed lake they parked, left the car to walk to the water's edge – bread in tow. They were alone here. Not another soul shared their impulse to come here this afternoon, Laurie thought with pleasure. They tossed bread crumbs to the delighted ducks. Neil reminisced about feeding the seagulls on the Montauk beach.

'This is the perfect time of year at Montauk,' he told her – his eyes making love. 'It's a haul, but let me take you there one weekend soon. I know you'll love it. This long stretch of pristine beach, and nobody there this time of year except for the seagulls and an occasional town dog.'

'It sounds lovely.' Her heart was pounding as she visualized walking on a deserted beach with Neil. But he talked about spending the weekend there—

'You're lovely,' he whispered, reaching for her. 'You know how I feel about you.' His eyes were asking urgent questions.

'Let's don't rush,' she said unsteadily, and then was silent as his mouth reached for hers and his arms pulled her close. The loaf of bread in her hands fell to the grass while the ducks quacked in reproach.

Laurie sat down to her solitary dinner in a blend of euphoria and doubt. Part of her was rejecting everything she'd considered important to her future. Was she making a terrible mistake? Yet how could she turn away from Neil after this afternoon?

Don't think about that now, she exhorted herself – eating without tasting. The task before her this evening was to write her letter 'to the Editor' of the *Enquirer*. Neil thought she should wait to see if someone else took on denouncing the cancellation of the concert. But now was the time to strike – with the subject so alive.

Pondering over what to write as she finished her dinner, she asked herself if she could persuade Neil to sign the letter along with her. He was third generation Bentonville. He was very popular in town.

But almost immediately her mind rejected asking him to join her in this campaign. She mustn't do anything to jeopardize his position in this town. His friends thought that he should run for the city council, eventually run for mayor.

I mustn't involve him in anything hurtful.

The dishes washed and dried, she sat down at her Royal portable to compose her letter to Jim Peters. She mustn't come across as angry, she exhorted herself. She must plead with readers to understand that to condemn Boris Kerensky on the basis of rumors was against American principles. What about 'innocent until proven guilty'?

People in Bentonville must realize what a horrible mistake had been made in canceling the concert. It said so blatantly that the foundations of this country were being violated. What happened to Boris Kerensky could happen to anybody – on the whim of any unthinking person. That was flouting democracy.

But some people – how many? – would

behave as badly as the HUAC down in Washington. When would Congress put a stop to this insanity?

And now there was that Republican senator – Joseph McCarthy – who was throwing around charges against top government officials. Each speech – and he made many – grew more rabid. He called Secretary of State Dean Acheson the 'Red Dean'. *Oh yes, I must write this letter.*

After endless revisions Laurie typed the final draft of her letter. Tomorrow afternoon she'd deliver it by hand to Jim Peters' office. Only then would she tell Neil what she had done.

Twelve

'No more stories,' Martha Madison told her young daughter with firmness but with deep affection. 'It's time to go to sleep. Todd's already asleep.' At eight Todd was three years Carol's senior.

'A little one?' Carol tried again, but her eyes conceded defeat.

'Martha,' her husband Sam called from the living room. 'Phone call for you.'

'I'll be right there—' She leaned forward to kiss Carol goodnight and to pull the light blanket over her daughter's small form.

She switched on the night light, hurried from the room – leaving the door slightly ajar, the way Carol liked. Walking into the living room, she understood from Sam's eloquent expression that this was a call she wouldn't particularly enjoy.

'Denise Spencer.' He mouthed the words.

Martha sighed, reached for the phone. Denise was apt to be long-winded and melodramatic about some fancied slight.

'Hello, Denise—'

'Martha, I'm so upset.' *She's always upset*

141

about something. 'It's about the new third grade teacher.'

'I hear the kids love her.' Martha was guarded.

'Oh, she makes it her business to win them over. She's here for no good – I'm sure of that!'

'I thought she was here for the pay check.' Martha chuckled. 'Not that it's the best paying job in town.'

'Everybody's talking. I've had half a dozen calls already.'

'About what?' Martha refused to be ruffled.

'The way she shot off her mouth about the committee's canceling the concert,' Denise shot back. 'Imagine having a teacher in our schools who goes out of her way to defend a Commie!'

'We don't know that.' Martha pantomimed her impatience to Sam.

'Of course we know that,' Denise rejected. 'She came right out and defended that Kerensky character to Doris Lowell. And that's not all. She's been making strange remarks to people around town.'

'I'll bring you a cup of tea,' Sam whispered to Martha. He suspected, Martha understood, that Denise would talk forever.

'I think you ought to bring it up at the School Board meeting at the end of the week,' Denise rushed on. 'We have an

142

obligation to the school system to make sure people don't infiltrate our classrooms.'

'Denise, you're getting upset over nothing. You—'

'Do you want your children to bc taught by some woman planted in the classroom by the Communist Party? I know my boys are both in high school – they're beyond her. But think of all the younger kids'

'Denise, we have no proof that Laurie Evans is a Communist,' Martha began.

'After what she said?' Denise broke in.

'To whom?' Martha countered. 'To Doris Lowell?'

'And others. Doris is terribly upset.'

'From what I hear, Doris is upset that Neil Winston is seeing the new teacher,' Martha said drily. 'She's building something totally innocent into a big deal. It's what clear-thinking people are calling a witch-hunt.'

Denise Spencer left the living room. Her husband Tom was engrossed in the World Series on television. She loathed baseball. She loathed the way Tom became a fanatic each year during the World Series. It was as though the future of the world was determined by the outcome.

And why was it necessary to have the volume so absurdly high? She walked into their bedroom and closed the door. In a corner of her mind she still fumed over

Martha Madison's reaction to what Doris had said about Laurie Evans. She sat on the edge of her bed, reached for the phone. Talk to Doris.

'Hello.' Doris's voice responded on the third ring.

'Doris, it's me,' Denise said. 'I'm so upset. I just talked with Martha Madison. You know she's on the School Board.'

'You told her about Laurie Evans defending Boris Kerensky?'

'Exactly! And you know her reaction?' Denise's voice grew shrill. 'She told me I was behaving hysterically. There was no way she would believe Laurie Evans was a Commie sympathizer. She didn't want to hear a word against that woman.'

'The little bitch is sure to betray herself somewhere along the line,' Doris soothed. 'It'll all come out real soon.' She paused. 'But the School Board should look into her background. Those people usually leave a trail a mile wide.'

'But who's going to bring it up before the School Board?' Denise demanded, then continued before Doris could reply. 'My sister Joyce's husband is a big advertiser with the *Record*. You know – ads for his store.' Excitement spiraled in her. 'I'll tell Joyce to talk to him about going to the *Record*, demanding a story about "troubles in our school system". When's the next board meeting?'

'Not for almost three weeks. But maybe we can push for an emergency meeting,' she said with new optimism. 'Giving the board time to do a background check before the regular meeting.'

'How would they do that?' Denise was uncertain.

'I'm not sure – but somebody on the board will know how to handle it. Whatever there is in her background that will label her a Commie sympathizer – or even a member of the Communist Party – will come out. Who else – besides Martha – do you know on the Board well enough to discuss this with? Denise, we can't just sit back and do nothing. Our school system is in jeopardy.'

Doris awoke the following morning with instant recall of her conversation last night with Denise. There must be somebody on the Board who'd understand the need for an emergency meeting. Denise and she were too upset last night to think straight. Surely Denise was friendly with somebody on the School Board other than Martha Madison – always so damn self-righteous. Somebody who could bring about an emergency meeting. As PTA president, Denise could demand an emergency meeting of the School Board.

It wouldn't be smart for *her* to be personally involved. Neil was infatuated by the little bitch. He'd be furious at whoever brought the matter out in the open. But Denise could do it. She was forever poking her nose into civic situations. And she could be very charming when she chose to be. What about her contacting Cynthia Andrews? Cynthia was chairman of the Board.

Doris glanced at the clock. It was just past 7 a.m. Wait until a few minutes past 8 – when Tom was leaving for his office. There was time for her to talk with Denise before she left for school. Remind Denise about calling her sister. The *Record* was always looking for a strong story for the front page – they probably wouldn't even need much prodding from Denise's brother-in-law to run a story about the Commie influence in the schools. And bring up contacting Cynthia Andrews.

At 7:53 a.m. Doris phoned Denise.

'Hello—' Denise sounded harried. Alarm welled in Doris. Had she discussed this with her husband and he'd told her to 'butt out' – as he was known to do on occasion?

'Has Tom left for the office yet?' Doris asked.

'He just walked out the door.' Denise understood. She wouldn't try to discuss anything important until Tom was out of the house. He was always making snide remarks about Denise's 'romance with the telephone'.

'I couldn't fall asleep until after midnight last night.' Doris sighed. 'I'm going to be exhausted by lunch time. But I've been so disturbed about what's happening at the school.' She hesitated. 'Did you talk with Tom about it?'

'Not yet. He was in a rotten mood about the ballgame last night.'

'I've given this a lot of thought, Denise. I know our only close contact on the School Board is Martha – and she's useless. But in these circumstances – and you can be so persuasive when it's important – you could call up Cynthia Andrews. She's chairman. Explain that some urgent information about a new teacher has come to your attention. She knows you're president of the PTA – it's natural for you to approach her. Tell her that once she's heard this, she'll see the need to call an emergency meeting. You'll—'

'I don't know, Doris.' Denise exuded alarm. 'Cynthia Andrews is so – so formidable.'

'And so powerful,' Doris pounced. Cynthia's husband Ralph was president of the Bentonville Bank. They owned half the property in town. 'You can handle this. You have a way with people like Cynthia Andrews.'

'I'll give it a try,' Denise said reluctantly.

'This morning, Denise. We can't waste time. And I'm calling Sally Mitchell. She's steaming at the way Laurie vilified her committee. I'll tell her to complain to Franklin about how everybody's furious that we have a Commie teaching in our school. He'll run to the School Board. Let's hit the Board from every direction.'

Betsy Mitchell glanced up from her bowl of hot cereal as her mother put down the phone.

'Mommy, when are you and Daddy going to give me a puppy?' It was a frequent, wistful plea.

'When you're a little older.' Sally Mitchell repeated her usual response.

A dog could create such havoc in a house, Sally thought in revulsion – though Donald looked with favor on such an acquisition. Dogs made a mess. She shuddered at the vision of a puppy cavorting about her pristine living room, with its white sofa and loveseat, her collection of fragile bric-à-brac.

'Finish your breakfast, Betsy,' she ordered. Betsy wouldn't be happy when she learned this morning's schedule. But Doris was right. They had to rid the school of a bad element.

'Mommy, we have to leave for school soon, don't we?' Betsy inspected the large, circular clock that hung over the gas range. 'I've never been late,' she reminded with pride.

'You won't be going to school today.' Sally geared herself for trouble. 'Dorothy comes to clean this morning. You'll stay here with her while I drive over to the school. You like Dorothy,' she reminded, her smile cajoling.

'Why won't I go to school?' Betsy frowned in bewilderment. 'Why are you going?' An accusing note in her voice now.

'I have a nine o'clock appointment with Mr Franklin.' Sally avoided Betsy's eyes, geared herself for what must be said. 'I'm asking Mr Franklin to transfer you into another third grade class.'

'I don't want to be transferred!' Betsy wailed. 'I love Miss Evans!'

'But she's a bad person.' Sally glowered in recall. 'I won't have my child exposed to somebody like her.'

'She's not bad!' Betsy screeched in outrage. 'I won't go to anybody else's class! I want to be in Miss Evans' class. Everybody likes her. She makes school fun.'

'I have to do what I think is right for you, Betsy. I know Mr Franklin will understand how important this is.'

Maybe it isn't enough to move Betsy from that woman's class. Maybe Miss Evans ought to be removed from the school. Talk to Carl Franklin

149

about reporting her to the School Board. The board can fire her.

Laurie reached for her jacket, purse, and tote. It was the beginning of another school day, but instinct warned her that once her letter appeared in the *Enquirer* she'd experience some friction in this town. Mr Peters would run the letter, wouldn't he?

Now doubts invaded her. Neil said the *Enquirer* hovered at the edge of extinction at regular intervals. Would Mr Peters be afraid that her letter would be too controversial? But surely he'd understand how important it was to stop this witch-hunting in their own town.

Closing her apartment door, she turned to look across the road. This was one of the days Neil left for school at the normal time – no early morning group at the school.

'Hi.' Neil called to her and waved.

'It's almost Indian summer again.' Why did her heart always begin to pound this way every time she saw Neil approaching? What did she truly know about his way of thinking? an inner voice mocked. Would he be like so many men – the ones who expected their wives to be satisfied to run a house and raise kids? His mother had done just that, the voice proceeded to taunt – until her husband had died and she'd gone to work to support herself and Neil.

'I've been thinking about the next mini-vacation at school.' Neil fell into step beside her. 'I mean, more than just a weekend.'

'Thanksgiving,' she pinpointed.

'Mom always makes a big deal out of Thanksgiving. We have maybe a dozen at the table. You know, unattached people who'll be on their own. You'll have Thanksgiving dinner with us, of course. And—'

'I'll be going down to New York for Thanksgiving dinner with my brother and sister-in-law. Just for the day,' she added in sudden decision. Tim and Iris wouldn't mind if she didn't stay for the whole weekend. She waited expectantly for Neil to continue.

'I was thinking that Friday the two of us could drive out to Montauk.' His eyes made ardent love to her. 'It's a long haul, I know – but there's a great place to stay out there. Gurney's Inn – right on the ocean. And I hear the food is great.'

'I know you love Montauk—' She was torn. Was she ready to make this kind of commitment? A tingling low within her told her she was.

'Long walks on a stretch of empty beach, the seascape a masterpiece in gray,' he cajoled. 'A charming little village that looks like a bit of New England in autumn. You'll love it.'

'I'll come back late Thanksgiving evening,'

she decided on impulse. 'We can drive out on Friday morning.' All at once she was uncomfortable. 'What will your mother think of us?'

Neil reached for her hand – his face alight with laughter. 'Don't you know by now? She's dying to become a mother-in-law. And she won't be shocked,' he joshed. 'The war years made a lot of changes in people's thinking. And Mom knows I'm in love with you, that I want us to be married. All right, I know – it's been such a short while since we met. But we'll wait. In my heart I knew that first day that I wanted to spend the rest of my life with you.'

'Neil, I'm not sure where I want to go with my life,' she stammered. She wanted to be an independent woman, one who made her own decisions. She wanted to go out into the world and be an equal human being – not the 'little woman'.

'No rush,' he soothed. 'I'm thirty-one – I've waited this long, I can wait a little longer. The prize is worth it,' he murmured, and made a point of not releasing her hand when they passed neighbors they both knew.

When they arrived at the school, Laurie was conscious of covert glances. It was all over town, she surmised, that 'Neil Winston is going with Laurie Evans, the new third grade teacher'. *Why am I pleased about this?*

I told him – didn't I? – that I wasn't ready to make any permanent commitment.

Carl Franklin glanced up with a martyred smile when the school secretary told him that Mrs Mitchell had arrived to see him, per her phone conversation.

'Give me five minutes to settle in, then send her in,' he instructed. Sally Mitchell was a pain in the ass, he reminded himself. Ever since her kid was in kindergarten, she'd had problems to report. What now? She'd read something in one of those weird magazines about how to run a classroom – and Bentonville Elementary wasn't doing just that?

It wasn't enough he had that nutty mother with the kid who broke her leg when another kid pushed her down to contend with – demanding the school pay the medical bills. Now Sally Mitchell was in a tizzy about something. How did her husband stay married to that nut case?

He glanced up at the faint knock at the door that told him Sally Mitchell was about to be ushered into his office.

'Mrs Mitchell, how nice to see you.' His smile was warm. His eyes were guarded.

'Oh, Carl, drop the formality,' she chided. 'I was always Sally when I worked with you on that fundraising committee last year.'

'Sally.' Now his smile was fatuous. Damn,

153

he hated the games you had to play with these stupid mothers. 'What brings you here this morning? Not that I'm not delighted to see you.'

'I've been hearing disturbing things about Betsy's teacher, Miss Evans.' Her face tightened.

The new third grade teacher again?

'First – in Betsy's presence – she carried on about how awful it was for the Arts League Committee to cancel the Kerensky concert next month. She called the committee's behavior shameful. We all know about his Commie connections. It was the committee's responsibility to keep that man out of our town. Then Denise Spencer called me.'

'Oh?' Franklin tried to conceal his annoyance. Spencer was another one always coming up with nutty proposals about 'what's best for our children'. She felt so damned important since she'd got herself elected president of the PTA.

'Denise, too, heard that Miss Evans is very outspoken about where her sympathies lie. She talks blatantly in front of her students. Several mothers are furious.'

'Miss Evans came to us with fine credentials.' He didn't need this, he thought irritably. 'She was in the top five per cent in college and graduate school. She speaks three languages and—'

154

'Including Russian?' Sally demanded. 'Denise talked to Martha Madison about calling an emergency meeting of the School Board next week, but Martha was against it. You know what she and her husband are like. They're spearheading that drive for a rise in property taxes.' Franklin's groan was eloquent. 'But if you talk to the board members, they'll listen to you. They'll probably call an emergency meeting. We can't afford to have a woman like that teaching our young, impressionable children.'

'I'll look into it,' Franklin promised. 'I suspect this is just some misunderstanding.' He glanced at his watch. 'I'll be in touch.'

Carl Franklin sat at his desk in deep thought. He felt a rush of anxiety. Could there be something in what Sally Mitchell said? It would be a horrible reflection on him if he'd hired a teacher who turned out to be a Commie.

When you get down to brass tacks, what do I know about this Evans woman, beyond her educational recommendations? Hell, I couldn't come out and say, 'What are your political affiliations?' But with people talking, I've got to do something.

Where do I go from here?

Thirteen

Cynthia Andrews sat in her small office off the elegant Regency-style living room of her pseudo-Georgian house and focused on the account book before her. She frowned in annoyance when the house phone – as opposed to her office phone – rang in the living room.

'Lottie, will you get that?' she called to her housekeeper, at that moment vacuuming in the foyer.

'Yes ma'am,' Lottie called back and went to respond to the ringing. 'The Andrews residence, good morning,' she chirped as directed by her employer. 'Oh, just a minute.'

'Well, who is it?' Cynthia asked. Long ago she'd made it clear to local people that she accepted phone calls only after business hours. Why was it so hard for people to realize that she ran a business from her home? She hadn't been playing at being an interior decorator all these years. It was her profession.

'Miz Spencer,' Lottie reported. 'Are you home?'

'She knows that now,' Cynthia snapped and rose to go to the phone. 'Hello, Denise—'

'Cynthia, I'm so sorry to disturb you,' Denise apologized, 'but something has arisen that should be brought to your attention. As the head of the elementary school PTA it's my duty, of course, to report serious problems to the Board of Ed. I've just—'

'Denise, I'm in the middle of a consultation with a client,' Cynthia lied. 'Why don't you drop by Friday morning – around ten o'clock? We can discuss it then.' *She sounds rattled. What's the big problem now that the Board of Ed has to handle?*

'Oh, all right. I'll be over on Friday around ten.'

Cynthia returned to her office. She'd been on the Board for almost seventeen years. Why did Ralph insist that she always go for re-election? Both boys had been out of the school system for years. One in law school now, the other in pre-med. But Ralph had this weird conviction that it was their civic duty to be active in these things.

Why had Denise Spencer decided to call her about whatever silly problem had arisen now? Because she was the chairman, she instantly concluded. Had any of the others been contacted? Denise had a sly streak in her. She reached for the phone on her desk.

Call Fred Robbins. Ask if he's heard anything about trouble in the school. What was the big problem last year? Oh yes, some mothers were upset that evolution was being discussed in a high school class.

Carl Franklin found it difficult to focus on the business at hand this morning. He kept hearing Sally Mitchell's voice: *'Denise, too, heard that Miss Evans is very outspoken about where her sympathies lie. She talks blatantly in front of her students. Several mothers are furious.'*

If mothers were talking, he'd have to take some action, he finally convinced himself. Who on the Board should he contact? Not Martha Mitchell. Not Jason Smith. Neither would go along with firing Evans. They wouldn't even give him credit for discovering the danger she represented. Gil Taylor, he decided with an air of relief. Taylor was a no-nonsense guy.

He reached for his phone book, tracked down Taylor's business number. He ran the major plumbing firm in the county. Even stocked bidets, Carl thought with a flicker of amusement – not that he ever sold one in this town.

He waited impatiently for Gil Taylor to come on the line.

'Yeah, Carl?' Gil's voice came to him. He knew this wasn't casual conversation – not during business hours.

'We've got a nasty situation at the school,' Carl reported and briefly outlined the situation.

'Wow!' Gil whistled in astonishment. 'I never expected to hear something like that in our classrooms.'

'It's almost three weeks till the next Board meeting. Don't you think it would be a good idea to call an emergency meeting? I mean, before this gets out of hand. First, we're almost entertaining that Commie pianist in town. Now this—'

'I'll need a little time to look into it.' Gil cleared his throat. Stalling before making a decision, Carl interpreted. Gil always liked to know which way the wind was blowing before he made a decision.

'Not too long,' Carl said pointedly.

'I'll give you a buzz over the weekend,' Gil promised. 'I'll talk to one or two other Board members. But we won't let this ride. If it's true, it's a damned serious situation.'

Today Laurie was impatient for class to be over. After school she'd go straight over to the *Enquirer*'s office, try to speak personally to Jim Peters. She felt recurrent guilt that she was taking this step without first telling Neil. But instinct told her he'd try to dissuade her from taking the letter to Peters just yet. Why couldn't Neil understand the urgency of the situation? He had Tim's way of sitting back to study any serious situation – but there were times when delay was dangerous. This was one of those times.

She felt a rush of relief when the bell rang for the end of the school day. Nobody lingered in the classroom because – after a sunny autumn morning – rain was beginning to fall. The sky was ominous, with dark gray clumps hinting at a thunderstorm. Today, she remembered, Neil was having a special meeting with his drama group. She'd head straight for the *Enquirer* office.

She reached into a storage closet for the umbrella she kept there for unexpected showers, hurried from her room and down the hall to the entrance. A sharp chill in the air prompted her to button her jacket as she emerged from the school. She geared herself for a meeting with Jim Peters. He might be busy. He might be away from his office. Then she'd just leave the letter for him. But intuition told her the letter would be more effective if she could speak to the newspaper editor in person.

She hurried from the school, strode towards Main Street. The *Enquirer* occupied a small red-brick structure at the far end of the business area, she recalled. The rain was threatening to become a downpour. Puddles appeared here and there. What was it Tim used to say? 'Good things happen on rainy days.' Let it be true.

She knew from reading the *Enquirer* that Jim Peters was a man of strong opinions. And thus far she'd agreed with his opinions. Yet she realized, too, that it would take a strong editor to throw his newspaper into the insanity that threatened the town.

She walked past the now familiar shops along Main Street without seeing. Let Jim Peters understand what was happening. Let him see the need to run her letter. Instinct told her there would be replies – both scathing and approving. But the problem would be out in the open. That was the important objective.

In his small, cluttered office at the *Enquirer* Jim Peters finished up a meeting with his accountant.

'That brings us up to date,' the accountant said with satisfaction and rose to leave. 'Except for my bill,' he added, grinning. 'Take care of that as soon as you can.'

'It's a promise.'

Jim felt a little less pressured than on most occasions. The newspaper was out of the red, showed a small profit. Admittedly, this had happened at regular intervals during the fourteen years he'd been running the paper. But this time he felt something more substantial in the wind. Local people were realizing the newspaper was fighting for their best interests.

Sara never complained, but he felt guilty that so much of the time they were surviving on her salary as the high school's guidance counselor. She chafed under the restrictions laid down by the powers-that-be, but she couldn't afford to quit until the newspaper was on firmer ground.

Damn, I'm fifty-one-years-old. It's time I was able to support my wife in a decent style. If we'd had kids – and we'd both longed for them – I couldn't have indulged myself this way. But Sara believed in me. Bless her for that. Maybe at last this is the turning point.

'Jim, somebody to see you.' His secretary punctured his introspection. 'A Laurie Evans.'

'Who's Laurie Evans?' He glanced up with an indulgent smile. 'What's she selling?'

'She's the new third grade teacher. She wants to talk to you about a letter she's written to the paper.' Helen – with him since the first day the *Enquirer* published – smiled. 'She's real pretty.'

Jim grinned. 'I won't hold that against her. Okay, send her in.'

He glanced up with a smile as Laurie walked into his office. Good thing she was teaching third grade. At high school level she'd have male hormones in an uproar.

'You want to talk to me.' His eyes were appraising. Bright, he decided before she'd said a word. A fighter – that came through loud and clear.

'Yes. We have a problem in town that I think has to be brought out into the open.'

'Sit down and tell me about it.' He was always ready for a good fight.

'It's about the cancellation of the Arts League concert,' she began and launched into a passionate denunciation of this decision.

Damn, she's right. But this could tear the town apart if we start taking sides. 'You've set this down in letter form?'

'Right here—' She brought an envelope from her purse, handed it to him. 'I think it's terribly important that this be brought out into the open. People have to recognize this is against everything this country believes in.'

She was nervous, he summed up as he read the letter, but determined to put up a fight.

'It's a fine letter,' he conceded. Sure to evoke strong feelings on both sides. But how could he run it without putting the newspaper in jeopardy? He decided on candor. 'I believe the way you do. It was a disgrace to the town – to cancel the concert on the strength of stupid rumors. But there'll be some people in town who'll be furious if I run your letter. I could lose some major advertisers. Right now I can't afford that.'

163

He managed a wry smile. 'You probably know by now, the *Enquirer* operates on a shaky financial foundation. We're always hanging on the edge.'

'You mean you won't run it?' Her eyes defied him to confirm this.

'I'll think about it, Laurie. I'm on your side – but it won't help anything if I find myself so short of advertisers that I can't pay my bills. I'll give it serious thought,' he promised because she looked so crushed. 'Let me think about it over the weekend. Call me Monday morning.'

Sara Peters knew as soon as Jim walked into the house that he was fighting an inner battle.

'What's for dinner?' he asked in his interested manner – after the usual quick buss and a pat on her rear.

'Pot roast.' Most dinners consisted of food that wouldn't be spoiled if Jim was late getting home – which happened frequently. 'With mashed potatoes and carrots.'

'Carrots again,' he grumbled good-humoredly, and hurried on before she could reply. 'I know, carrots are good for the eyes.'

'I'll get dinner on the table.' When he was ready, he'd spill what was bothering him.

'How was school today?' he asked belatedly.

'The normal small problems,' she shrugged, headed into the kitchen. It was a mistake, she thought for the hundredth time, to have Carl Franklin act as principal for both the elementary grades and the high school. But good for the school budget, she thought with a sigh.

Over dinner Sara reported on local news that had drifted her way in the course of the day. Waiting for him to open up about what was troubling him. Then – serving himself another helping of pot roast – he came out with it.

'Damn it, Sara, did you hear about the Kerensky concert being canceled?'

'How could I not hear about it?' she countered. 'It's a major topic of conversation in town.' She sighed. 'I'd been looked forward to it.' She was the *Enquirer*'s music critic – a role she relished. 'But don't tell me you're all upset at missing it?' she joshed. 'Half the time you fall asleep at the concerts.'

'Only when I've been on a twelve-hour shift for a few days.' He paused. She waited for him to continue. 'The new teacher at the school thinks it was a rotten thing for the committee to do.'

'She's a music lover?' Questions tugging at her. *What's bothering Jim this way?*

'She's upset that the man's concert was canceled on the basis of rumors. This nutty Red Scare!' He grunted with contempt.

165

'She's right,' Sara agreed. 'The way I hear it, he was canceled over in Linwood – so our high-minded committee decided they should do the same. They have no real basis for canceling.'

'Laurie Evans – she's the new teacher – came into my office this afternoon. She'd written a letter about the situation. She didn't want to just mail it in – she wanted to talk to me about it. To make sure I'd run it. A real firebrand letter. You know what an uproar that would start in town if I ran it.'

'You've never been afraid of that before.' Her eyes held his.

'Sara, for the first time the newspaper is out of the red. How the hell can I throw away everything we've worked for all these years because a concert was canceled in this town?'

'It's lots more than a canceled concert.' Sara's eyes were eloquent.

'I know that!' He scowled in reproach. 'But I never expected the Commie nuttiness to sneak into our own town.'

'There were small towns all over Germany that probably felt the same way. "The Nazis are in Berlin, the big towns. They won't affect us."' She hesitated. 'What are you going to do? Are you going to run the letter?'

'I don't know,' he admitted. 'I just don't know.'

166

Fourteen

Laurie spent a restless evening. She knew that Neil was with his drama group at school – in heavy rehearsal for their first performance of the season. When he hadn't called by ten o'clock, she prepared for bed. He would be angry that she'd gone ahead and taken her letter to Jim Peters, she warned herself. He'd wanted her to wait a bit. But it was necessary to act now.

She'd just settled herself in bed with a book when the phone rang. She left the bed, hurried to answer. Knowing the caller would be Neil.

'Hello?' Faintly breathless from anticipation that blended with guilt. Couldn't Neil understand that she'd had to go to Jim Peters?

'We had a long rehearsal,' he said, but he was pleased. 'The kids are working so hard.'

'Neil, you know the letter I mean to take to Peters at the *Enquirer*?' She took a deep breath, gearing herself for reproach. 'Well, I did. I mean, I wrote it last night and this afternoon I took it to him.'

For a moment silence. 'Is he going to run it?' Neil sounded anxious, Laurie thought. 'You talked to him about it?'

'We talked. He – he sounded ambivalent,' she admitted. 'He said he believed the way I do – but he's nervous about the reaction of advertisers. He said he had to think about it. He told me to call him Monday morning.'

'Jim knows some readers will be sympathetic – but others will be furious. He kind of walks a tightrope a lot of the time. He tries to present what he feels is right, yet he realizes he can stay in business only as long as he has enough advertising to keep him solvent. Talk with him on Monday.' Neil dismissed this, yet Laurie sensed he was uneasy. 'Why don't we go to the drive-in Friday evening? They're showing *All The King's Men*. I hear it's marvelous. It won the Academy Award. We'll have dinner at the house, then head for the drive-in,' he plotted.

'That sounds great.' She struggled to sound enthusiastic. *Neil's upset. He thinks the letter was a bad move.*

Off the phone she debated about calling Tim and Iris. No. Tim was forever saying that she acted before thinking things through. But she had thought this through. It was a terrible mistake to cancel the Kerensky concert!

168

The moment she walked into the school the next morning Laurie was conscious of an odd undercurrent. Not that anything was said, she analyzed. But she sensed that she'd been the subject of heated discussion in the past dozen hours. It came through in veiled glances from those she encountered en route to her classroom. Nobody could know about her letter to the *Enquirer*. Mr Peters wouldn't have talked about it to anyone else. What was happening?

At lunch time in the cafeteria she was aware of covert scrutiny. *Oh, I'm being melodramatic. What could have happened overnight?* Determined not to succumb to inchoate alarm, she paid the cashier and headed for the lunchroom.

Karen was already seated at their table. She glanced up with a welcoming smile as Laurie approached.

'Wouldn't it be nice if the cafeteria didn't stick to the same menu each day of the week?' Karen said philosophically. No sign that anything was wrong, Laurie comforted herself. She was imagining situations that didn't exist. 'I'd like to know that on Thursdays the hot dish wasn't always meat loaf and mashed potatoes.'

'That letter we talked about—' Laurie glanced about, lowered her voice. 'You know, my letter to the *Enquirer*—' She took a deep breath. 'I wrote it – and I took it to

Mr Peters.' All at once Karen seemed tense. 'Don't tell anybody else. He agreed with what I said, only he was ambivalent about running it. I'm to call him Monday morning.'

'Wow!' All at once Karen frowned, warning in her eyes. Pat and Sharon were approaching. Laurie understood; this wasn't to be discussed with them. 'Hi,' Karen greeted the other two teachers. 'Did you hear the news this morning about Korea?'

A safe subject to discuss, Laurie interpreted. Yet she intercepted an odd exchange between Pat and Sharon. She wasn't wrong. Something – concerning her – had happened. Instinct told her she was right.

She was relieved when the school day was over. As usual on those days when he had no after-school groups, Neil was waiting for her in the lobby. Instantly she was aware that he, too, sensed something unusual was in the air. Was it just that people were talking about Neil and her? Did they resent his involvement with the new teacher in town? Maybe that was it, she told herself. So be it.

'Let's go over to The Oasis for coffee,' he suggested with a warm smile. 'I hear they make a terrific cheese Danish.' His eyes told her he was aware of the covert glances from a pair of fellow teachers whom she knew only by sight.

That was it, she told herself again. People were gossiping about Neil and her.

Laurie awoke on Friday morning with an immediate recall that she and Neil were going to the drive-in tonight. First they'd have dinner at his house. It was so pleasant there, his mother so sweet and affectionate. Were Tim and Iris becoming aware of the place Neil was filling in her life? She always realized – after they'd talked – that Neil's name kept creeping into her conversation. They'd like Neil.

Despite the craziness about the concert being canceled, she felt that Bentonville was a good town. *I'm glad I came here. It's the best move I've ever made.*

Fortified by a mug of strong black coffee, Jim Peters gazed at the front page of the *Enquirer* with some misgivings. Sara had got through to him last night – as usual. He'd decided to run Laurie Evans' letter, even though his mind warned this was a hazardous thing to do. But wasn't he thumbing his nose at those who'd disapprove when he positioned it in the center of the first page?

Hell, Laurie's right. This town needs to be awakened to what's happening right in its midst.

He swigged down the last of his coffee, checked his watch. It was past 7 a.m. She'd be awake by now. She'd be damned happy to know the letter was in print.

'Chuck!' he yelled and their new office boy – full of enthusiasm at being part of a newspaper – jogged into view.

'Yes, sir?'

'Take this newspaper over to Laurie Evans' house.' He scrawled her address at the top of the front page. 'She has an apartment there,' he recalled. 'Use the side entrance.'

Jim leaned back in his chair when Chuck had dashed off to deliver the copy of the *Enquirer* to Laurie Evans and considered his actions. Some of his ultra-conservative advertisers were going to be mad as hell when they read this morning's newspaper. But hadn't he opened his own newspaper so he'd have the freedom to say what he thought? He printed what was good for this town. What Laurie Evans had to say was good for Bentonville.

Laurie emerged from the shower, reached for a towel, shivered at the chill of the bathroom. Instinct warned her that the Kendricks would be ever slow in providing sufficient heat. She dressed hurriedly, went out to the kitchen to put up breakfast.

The sound of the doorbell startled her. She glanced at the clock en route to the door. Who'd be here at 7:28 a.m.? A tele-

172

gram? Alarm welled in her. Had something happened to Tim or Iris?

Her heart pounding she reached for the door, pulled it wide.

'Miss Evans?' the boy in his late-teens at the door asked with an engaging smile.

'Yes.'

'Mr Peters told me to bring you a copy of this morning's *Enquirer.*'

'Oh, thank you.'

He dashed away before she could offer a tip. She opened the paper wide, prepared to flip to the 'Letters to the Editor' page. But that wasn't necessary. In the middle of the front page – above a small article – the words 'LOCAL TEACHER LAMENTS WITCH-HUNTING IN BENTONVILLE' emblazoned its contents.

'Oh, my God!' Simultaneously astonished and elated, she devoured the copy. Mr Peters had run every single word.

She reached for the phone. Neil was going to be upset, she warned herself yet again.

'Hello?' His voice came to her with an edge of wariness. He, too, was conscious of the early hour for a phone call.

'Neil, Mr Peters just sent over a copy of this morning's *Enquirer.* I can't believe it! He ran my letter. Not on the "Letters to the Editor" page. On the front page!'

'Laurie, hold it a moment.' She heard him in conversation with his mother. She, too, was concerned at this early morning call. 'Laurie' – he came back to her – 'why don't you come over and have breakfast with us? Mom's putting up pancakes now. And bring the *Enquirer*,' he added with an air of urgency.

'I'll be right there,' she agreed. *Neil is upset*. But Mr Peters had agreed with her, she told herself defensively. If this went by unchallenged, how could they know what would happen next?

Neil was at the door as she approached. Despite his welcoming smile, he radiated concern. He was sorry she'd written the letter. He regretted that Mr Peters had decided to run it. The word would spread around town fast. So a lot of people didn't subscribe to – or read – the *Enquirer*. Those who did – approving or not – would be burning up the phone lines this morning.

'The coffee's perking, and Mom's about ready to bring pancakes to the table,' he told her.

The aroma of coffee permeated the house as Laurie walked inside. There was a faint whiff of heat coming up – though this was early in the season. The warmth provided an atmosphere of sybaritic comfort.

In silence Laurie handed Neil the newspaper, searched his face as he read. Was she wrong about Neil? Had she given him qualities in her mind that didn't truly exist?

'Jim has guts,' Neil commented as he read while they walked back to the kitchen. 'This is sure to cost him advertisers.'

'Read Laurie's letter to me,' his mother commanded as they arrived in the kitchen.

Beth listened absorbedly while Neil read – all the while flipping pancakes from grill to plate.

'You did the right thing, Laurie,' she approved. 'You'll wake this town up to what's happening.'

But Neil was so somber. Was her letter erecting a barrier between them? His mother approved. Neil did not.

Denise was clearing the breakfast table – Tom off to the office – when the phone rang. Frowning in annoyance she went to respond. Since she had awoken, she'd been searching her mind for words to convince Cynthia Andrews that she must call an emergency meeting of the School Board.

'Hello?'

'It's me,' Doris said. 'Have you seen this morning's *Enquirer*?'

'I don't read that rag.'

'Nor do I normally,' Doris said. 'But this morning I did. Denise, you won't believe what's happening!'

Denise listened with rising rage while Doris read her Laurie Evans' letter to the *Enquirer*. Yet she felt a grim satisfaction –

175

here was back-up for what she had to tell Cynthia Andrews.

Denise waited impatiently for time to pass. At last she left the house, headed for her appointment with Cynthia Andrews. Oh, stop off in town and pick up a copy of the *Enquirer*. In face of Laurie Evans's letter with its flagrant display of her loyalties how could Cynthia not call an emergency meeting of the School Board?

The Board had the authority to dismiss a teacher. Maybe now Carl Franklin would have enough sense to hire Emily Pierce.

Fifteen

At Cynthia Andrews' house Denise was greeted by the housekeeper.

'Mrs Andrews asked that you wait for her in the living room. She's on the phone with a client.'

'Thank you.' Her smile was polite, but Denise was annoyed. Cynthia was always trying to make people think she was so important.

The rolled-up *Enquirer* in one hand, Denise sat on one corner of the Duncan Phyfe sofa in the living room of which Cynthia Andrews was so proud. She could hear Cynthia in animated conversation in the nearby office. Sometimes she suspected Cynthia thought she was doing people a favor just to live in this town.

'Now don't worry, Janice, the house will be finished by Thanksgiving. You'll have the housewarming as planned.'

Moments later Cynthia walked into the living room. She acted like a queen about to give an audience to a lowly subject, Denise thought as they exchanged greetings.

'Now what's the problem at the school?' Cynthia asked with a show of indulgence.

Denise gave her planned speech about Laurie Evans, then – with a dramatic gesture – unfolded the paper and handed it to Cynthia.

'This is the crowning touch. How dare she upbraid us for being honorable, decent citizens!'

Cynthia flinched in distaste as she read. 'I'm appalled! To say such things about our town!'

'She has to be removed from the school. I've spoken with a dozen mothers – all of them upset that their children are exposed to a Commie teacher. I'm horrified that something like this can happen here in Bentonville.'

Cynthia was grim. 'Oh yes, this calls for action.'

'An emergency meeting?' Denise prodded.

'Exactly. I'll call for an immediate meeting of the Board. On the weekend. We won't waste time.' Cynthia rose to her feet in dismissal. 'Thank you for bringing this to my attention, Denise.'

Laurie dreaded going into the cafeteria for lunch today. Arriving at school this morning, she'd felt hostility on every side. For a while she'd lost herself in classroom activities. No point in stalling, she admonished herself. Go to the cafeteria – just as on any other day.

She'd known there would be those who labeled her a troublemaker. She hadn't expected to feel all at once an outcast – there were those who agreed with her. She wasn't alone in her feelings about the cancellation of the concert.

It was so much more than that, she analyzed. Canceling the concert set a dangerous precedent. It said that rumor was to be accepted as truth. The old ruling of being innocent until proven guilty – beyond reasonable doubt – was dead in the minds of too many. She contrived a casual smile as she walked towards the cafeteria, took her place in line. Conscious again of hostility.

With her tray she headed towards the elementary teachers' lunchroom. Pat and Sharon were already seated at their usual table. She ignored nasty glances from nearby tables as she took her place across from Pat and Sharon.

'Hi.' She was determinedly cheerful. 'Another week almost down the hatch.'

'Yeah.' Pat seemed to be avoiding eye contact. 'This term seems to be racing past.'

'That's a new blouse, isn't it?' Sharon managed a tight little smile. 'It's very pretty.'

'Thank you.' Laurie's eyes shifted from Sharon to Pat. They both knew about the letter. They were both determined to ignore it. They were uncomfortable sitting here with her, she realized all at once. She glanced up with a flurry of relief as Karen arrived.

'That was very brave – a very necessary thing,' Karen said, sitting across from Laurie. 'Howie said he was proud of you.' Her eyes said she was aware of much disapproval.

'Why can't they serve something beside chicken soup for lunch?' Pat complained in a flurry of discomfort. 'It always tastes as though the chicken just ran through it.'

'Every once in a while I swear I'm going outside for lunch,' Sharon contributed, ignoring Laurie and Karen. 'But I never do—'

Now the conversation focused on the weather – unseasonably cool today. The atmosphere was supercharged. Pat and Sharon ate in haste, murmured inane excuses about not dawdling over lunch today. Laurie's eyes followed them as they rushed from the table.

'You should have expected that,' Karen said wryly yet with sympathy. 'Neither Pat nor Sharon is one to rock the boat.'

'I thought they were my friends.' That was naive of her, wasn't it? Laurie shook her head in bewilderment.

'Are you busy tonight?' Karen asked.

'Yes,' Laurie said, her eyes questioning.

'I'm going to Neil's house for dinner. Then we're going to the drive-in.' *Will he want to have me there for dinner tonight? Will he want to be seen with me at the drive-in?*

'What about Saturday night?' Karen pursued.

'Nothing definite.' She'd supposed she'd be seeing Neil.

'Come to dinner with Howie and me,' Karen said. 'I'll call Neil and ask him, too. Instinct tells me we need to talk. This craziness about your letter isn't going to just drift away. And remember, if you need an attorney, Howie's your boy.'

Jim Peters stared into space – one hand gripping the telephone while Clark Edmonds raged about the letter published on the *Enquirer*'s front page that morning.

'Jim, you were out of your mind to print that garbage! This town is incensed. So she was insane enough to write that letter – why were you crazy enough to print it?'

'What she wrote was true, Clark. Canceling that man was an outrage. We don't have to emulate that ridiculous committee down in Washington.'

'That committee is out to preserve this country's safety! Are you forgetting what's going on in Korea? I know, most people are. But Russia's behind the fighting in Korea. They're all fired up because this country passed a law against Communism!'

'It's my obligation to print what I feel is right for my readers.' Jim was perspiring now despite the coolness of the day. 'We can't go around letting people be hounded for no reason other than rumors.'

'I can't give my advertising to a newspaper that reviles my town! As of now my store runs no ads in the *Enquirer*!'

Jim flinched as the phone at the other end was slammed down with force. Hell, he'd known there'd be some repercussions, he reminded himself. He scowled when the phone rang again.

'Jim Peters—'

'Peters have you flipped your lid?'

Jim gritted his teeth while another advertiser reviled his editorial judgement. Hell, he'd known this would happen. All right, settle in for the battle.

Ten minutes later – after four more enraged callers had withdrawn their advertising in the *Enquirer* – Jim buzzed his secretary.

'No more calls, Helen. Say I've gone to Tahiti. You don't known when I'll be back.'

'As bad as that?' Helen tried for lightness, but concern seeped through.

'We've weathered other storms. We'll see this through,' he said with shaky confidence. 'So we'll have to chase a little harder for advertising.'

* * *

Laurie arrived at Neil's house before him. Beth greeted her with the usual warmth. At least, Beth was still on her side – along with Karen and Howie.

'Neil's still at school. He's working his butt off with the drama group,' Beth said. 'Come out to the kitchen and have a cup of coffee while we wait for dinner.'

'Everything smells so good.' Laurie sniffed appreciatively as they walked down the hall to the kitchen.

'My phone hasn't stopped ringing,' Beth confided while she poured coffee. 'I took it off the hook about an hour ago. Wouldn't you think people would leave you alone at least close to the dinner hour?'

'I ruffled a lot of feathers—' Beth agreed with her, but what about Neil? It disturbed her that he seemed upset that she'd gone ahead with the letter instead of waiting to see if someone else would bring up the subject.

'I've ruffled feathers in my time,' Beth said after a moment. 'I remember – during World War I – when the clamor for women's rights was growing louder by the day, and I went down to New York to be part of a suffragette parade.' Her eyes glowed in recall. 'Of course, my mother pretended to be furious with me – because my father was outraged by the idea of women going to the polls. But

I knew that in her heart she was proud of me.'

'My brother Tim is forever telling me I'm too impulsive. That I need to sit back and think before I jump into action.' *Neil thinks a lot like Tim. But I had to write that letter.*

'Laurie, sometimes you grow more cautious as you get older,' Beth conceded, then chuckled. 'Neil tells me that sometimes I act as though I am still eighteen. But sometimes I think that's good,' she added with a touch of defiance. 'I'm proud of you for writing that letter. I respect and admire Jim Peters for having the courage to run it. But—' She paused, frowning in thought.

'But what?' Laurie pursued, all at once uneasy.

'He's likely to lose advertisers. It's happened to him before – and he always bounces back.' Beth tried for an optimistic smile. 'It's just that keeping the paper alive has always been such a battle for him and Sara.'

Laurie was suddenly alert. 'Sara Peters? Is his wife the school's guidance counselor?'

'That's right. A nice woman.'

'Then she's the one I should talk to about Oliver.' Laurie's mind was racing. 'A little boy in my class,' she explained in answer to Beth's raised eyebrows. 'I know he's being abused at home. I went to Franklin, and he just brushed me aside—'

Beth nodded. 'It's not the school's responsibility to intervene in domestic problems,' she mimicked Franklin. 'Neil's run into that.'

'I'll drop by Sara Peters' office next week,' Laurie said with vigor.

'What are you seeing tonight?' Beth asked, her eyes compassionate.

'*All The King's Men.*' A great movie wasn't going to make her forget the atmosphere in this town. But somebody had to make people understand that what they were doing was dangerous.

'Oh, yes, Laurie – you remind me of myself at your age,' Beth said gently. 'Remember, it wasn't until August 1920 that women finally got the vote. I was twenty-five then. Ever since my early teens I'd been indignant that women couldn't vote. In some states women could vote, but not in federal elections until then. My father loved me, but he thought I was out of my mind. Women were to be nurtured and cherished – but to have the right to vote? That was absurd.'

'If nobody speaks out, then nothing happens.'

'Right. But remember, too' – Beth's smile was whimsical – 'even today there are women who don't bother to go to the polls.'

'I know – and I can't understand that!' Laurie blazed.

'You'll be seeing a lot of anger because of

185

your letter,' Beth conceded. 'It's the angry ones who're always heard. There are people who believe as you and I do – but they're the last to be heard.'

'But they will be heard. Bless Jim Peters for running my letter. Bless him for placing it where nobody who reads the *Enquirer* can miss it.'

'Mom?' Neil's voice came from the front of the house. 'I'm home.'

'Alice, did you see that letter in this morning's *Enquirer*?' Denise's voice was shrill over the phone. 'I couldn't believe Jim Peters could be so stupid as to run it!'

'You know I don't read that rag.' Alice's tone was scathing.

'Well, I don't read it, either. But then my mother does – and she called to tell me about it.'

A quarter mile away Clark Edmonds' wife was on the phone with her sister-in-law. 'Oh, I tell you, Peters will regret the day he ran that letter in his newspaper. On the front page yet. Clark's canceled all his advertising with the *Enquirer*. He's calling members of the Chamber of Commerce and urging them to do the same!'

While his wife waited in annoyance because dinner was ready to be served, Jason Smith listened in strained silence while Gil Taylor – another School Board member – seconded Cynthia Andrews' insistence that they meet in emergency session the following night.

'Come on, Jason,' Gil exhorted. 'Are we to sit back and do nothing when our very school rooms are being desecrated by some Commie teacher?'

'We don't know that she's a Communist,' Jason repeated for the third time. 'But all right, we'll meet tomorrow evening. But let's do it with a cool head.' Which wasn't likely, he warned himself. God, there were people in this country who expected the Commies to take over the nation.

Laurie approved of Beth's efforts over dinner to keep the conversation light.

'I don't want to hear about Korea,' she proclaimed. 'Let's forget about the House Un-American Activities Committee and that pig Senator Joe McCarthy,' Beth ordered.

'How are rehearsals on the play going?' Laurie asked Neil. *He seems so distracted. He's worried about my letter.*

'The kids are doing great,' he said with an effort to show enthusiasm. 'I'm not sure we have a future Paul Muni or Bette Davis, though,' he conceded.

'Oh, let me tell you Eric's latest brainstorm.' Beth's face brightened. 'He's making an addition to the store. He wants to have a special corner for children's books. And on Saturday mornings he plans a story-telling hour for the three-to-six group.'

'What's for dessert, Mom?' Neil was making an effort at casualness now.

'Your favorite bread pudding with the bourbon sauce.' Beth rose from the table. 'Coming right up.'

'We'll have to be leaving soon,' Neil told Laurie. 'The drive-in always starts right on the button.'

'Don't rush through your dessert,' Beth ordered. 'They always show a lot of garbage at the beginning. And my bread pudding deserves to be eaten slowly. Enjoy every bite.'

Laurie and Neil joined the long trail of cars headed for the drive-in with an awareness that not a star appeared in the sky. The moon played an in-and-out game with the clouds.

'Rain by early morning,' Neil predicted as he guided the car into a position far to one side. Already patrons were making a dash for the food concession – anxious to be provided before the main feature began. 'In the mood for popcorn or a soda?'

'After one of your mother's dinners?' Laurie scoffed. 'That would be sacrilegious.'

The feature began. Neil reached for

Laurie's hand. The drive-in area was clothed in darkness. The sliver of moon behind the clouds now. Laurie found it difficult to focus on the screen. It was a great picture – but she was too troubled to enjoy it.

She realized that Neil, too, was too tense to enjoy the film. *He's worried about me. He thinks I jumped in too fast. But how can we ignore what's happening in this town? My perfect small town.*

'Laurie, remember I love you,' he whispered, pulling her close in the shadows. 'I'm not trying to rush you – just reassure you,' he said with a touch of wry humor.

'I never thought I could feel this way about anybody,' she admitted. Relishing the comfort of his arms about her, the closeness of him. 'I can't wait for Thanksgiving weekend – when you're taking me to Montauk.'

'Do we have to wait?' His face against hers.

She fought against the impulse to say 'no'.

'Let's wait,' she pleaded. *I'm impulsive about so many things – but not about this.*

'You know, Laurie, all you have to do is say the word, and I'll take you by the hand and run with you to the marriage license window down at the courthouse.'

'It's been such a little while,' she whispered, though she knew that in the darkness of the car they were isolated from the rest of the world. 'A little more time, Neil. Please?'

'You make the rules,' he said tenderly.

Half an hour later – by mutual consent – they left the drive-in and headed for home. Approaching their block Laurie made a point of suggesting they go to his house. 'For some of your mother's wonderful coffee.' She didn't trust herself to be alone with Neil in her apartment. Nothing must spoil what they had found together. Now – with this ugliness in town – was the wrong time.

A porch light was on at the Winston house, though they were not expected for hours. They parked in the driveway, walked into the house. Beth was on the phone as they strolled into the living room. She seemed upset, Laurie noted – instantly alert.

'Thanks, Eric. I do appreciate your telling me.' Beth gestured to Neil and Laurie to sit down. 'This whole matter is ballooning into absurdity – but then we're living in odd times.' She listened for another moment. 'Sure, see you in the morning.' She put down the phone, took a deep breath.

'Problems, Mom?' Neil managed to sound casual but his eyes betrayed his anxiety.

'Eric said his cleaning lady was still there today when he got home from the office.' She turned to Laurie. 'Della comes in one day a week. Usually she's gone by the time Eric arrives from the shop, but she had to go to the school about one of her kids today and didn't get in until late and—'

'Mom, what did Eric tell you?' Neil broke in.

'Della ran out of furniture polish and ran over to the A&P to pick up a bottle. She bumped into her niece, who cleans for Nadine Taylor. Nadine told her that Cynthia Andrews has called an emergency meeting of the School Board tomorrow night. From the phone call she overheard, she said they were talking about – about removing the "Commie teacher" at the school.'

Sixteen

Laurie woke on Saturday morning with a sense of dread. This would be the longest weekend of her life, she thought with a shudder. Neil and Beth were convinced this emergency meeting of the School Board was an act of hysteria that sensible members of the Board would put to rest. But when she'd called Karen late last evening to bring her up to date, Karen had seemed shaken.

How could the School Board fire her? But the Arts League Committee had canceled Boris Kerensky's concert – with no real reason. If the School Board fired her, she'd have a terrible time trying to find another teaching position.

She'd have to leave Bentonville, she realized in sudden desolation. How could she marry Neil? She'd thought she was realizing a dream. She'd moved into a nightmare.

Reluctantly she prepared for the day. As usual she'd go to the A&P this morning to stock up on groceries. She'd drive over with Neil. Devoid of hunger, she forced herself to prepare and eat breakfast. She debated calling Karen again. No, she and Neil were going there for dinner tonight.

She was washing breakfast dishes when she heard thunder. Then lightning darted across the sky. There were times, she thought, when she loved to stand by a window and watch a storm take over the skies. This wasn't one of those days. The storm echoed the trauma in her life.

She started at the sound of the doorbell. Neil, she guessed with a flicker of pleasure, and went to the door.

'I dreamed of you last night,' he said, his eyes making love to her. Trying to ignore what this evening might bring. 'A great night—'

'Let's get to the supermarket before the crowds descend.' But her arms closed about his shoulders for a moment as he bent to kiss her. 'You know what it's like by ten o'clock.'

'Yes, ma'am.' He sighed eloquently. 'Grab your coat and let's make a dash for the car.' Already rain was pelting the earth.

At the A&P Laurie was instantly aware of belligerent glances. Only one early shopper waved a warm greeting to Neil, smiled in her direction.

'Who is she?' Laurie asked curiously as the friendly shopper strode towards the rear of the store. Somebody who probably didn't recognize her. It amazed her that so many people did know her by sight. But wasn't that one of the things she'd always liked about small towns? 'The woman who waved to you—'

'Oh, that's Martha Madison. She and her husband Sam are great. They worked with me when I was fighting for funds for the library.' He paused. 'She's on the School Board.'

'You mean I may have one friend?' Laurie flipped. 'She smiled at me.'

'Martha is a no-nonsense lady. She and Sam have two of the nicest kids. The older one is in one of my classes. Her husband is in real estate.'

'Neil—' Laurie fought for composure. 'Can the School Board fire me? I mean, is that their function?'

'In this town it is,' Neil conceded somberly. 'But this isn't a formal meeting tonight. Somebody got hot under the collar and called an emergency meeting.' He paused. 'There're seven people on the Board. They can't all be afflicted by this crazy hysteria.'

But how many Board members did it take, Laurie asked herself – all at once ice-cold – to throw her life into total chaos?

'Why the hell did you call your meeting for five p.m.?' Ralph Andrews asked his wife in irritation.

'Because they'd probably expect me to

serve them dinner if I'd suggested a later hour.' Cynthia's tone was acerbic. 'This way I'll serve cocktails and we'll settle down to business.'

'Not in the living room?' He grunted in disapproval

'In the den,' she told him. 'You'll be able to watch football.'

She frowned at the sound of the doorbell. 'One of them is always sure to be punctual.'

Lottie was at the door. Cynthia listened for a moment. 'Martha Madison,' she told Ralph. 'Mix cocktails for us – then you're off the hook.'

'You're always so punctual.' Cynthia greeted Martha Madison with the smile she reserved for people she viewed with wariness. Martha could be difficult. 'That's so rare these days.'

'It makes life easier.' Martha seemed casual, yet was suspect in Cynthia's eyes. 'Oh, somebody else is arriving.' They heard a car pull up outside. 'I assume this will be a short meeting?' It was a statement more than a question. Saturday evening in Bentonville was slated for socializing.

Cynthia bristled. 'An important meeting. I wouldn't have called it otherwise.'

Within five minutes all seven Board members were seated in the ostentatiously furnished den of the Andrews house. Ralph was serving martinis. In a corner of her mind Cynthia calculated the votes that would duplicate her own if they decided to throw out Laurie Evans without further investigation. But ten to one, she thought – already irritated at the prospect – Martha Madison and Jason Smith would put up a battle. It was a familiar pattern since the two of them had been voted on the Board.

Ralph placed the martini shaker at Cynthia's right and – with an arch smile – left the den. Cynthia launched into her prepared speech about the need for this meeting.

'I don't see how we can avoid taking some sort of action,' she wound up.

'Hell, everybody in town is in an uproar about this,' Gil Taylor reinforced. 'We can't just let it slide by.'

'To my understanding there's no proof that Miss Evans is a Communist sympathizer,' Martha Madison began calmly. 'And that holds for Boris Kerensky as well. I agree with her. It was a dreadful mistake to have canceled the concert on the strength of rumors.'

'Martha, don't be naive.' Cynthia frowned. 'Kerensky signed all kinds of petitions.' That was what they did, wasn't it? 'She was probably sent to this town as a spy. We know—'

'We know nothing,' Jason broke in. 'Can you specifically identify a petition Kerensky signed? Has the government offered any proof that he's a spy?'

'I have a suggestion.' Gil Taylor cleared his throat self-consciously. 'Let's set an investigation in motion. Not about Kerensky,' he stipulated. 'The Evans woman. Find out where she went to school. Where—'

'I have that right here.' Cynthia's smile was triumphant. 'I have the records of her application for the position in our school system. Carl Franklin was most cooperative. We—'

'If you're talking about hiring private investigators,' Martha Madison cautioned, 'that can cost an awful lot of money.'

'We have an emergency fund,' Cynthia reminded. 'According to my information—' She pulled pages from a folder at her left. 'Laurie Evans took her BA at Hunter College in New York. She earned her masters in education at Columbia University and—'

'Hey, we may have a short cut,' Ted Jackson interrupted with an air of excitement. 'When was she at Columbia?'

Cynthia inspected the papers before her. 'She received her masters degree just this past May.'

'Pay dirt!' Ted gloated. 'My wife's niece earned her masters at Columbia at the same time. I'll have Elaine phone and talk to her – she lives down in New York. Let's see what information she can dig up.'

'That's a wild goose chase,' Jason Smith scoffed. 'Have you any idea how many graduate students there are at Columbia? What are the odds that Elaine's niece ever even heard of her?'

'This woman has a big mouth.' Gil's eyes swept around the table. 'She's probably got a history of writing letters, speaking to groups, screeching the party line. I'll take any bet that she's left a trail a mile wide behind her. What have we got to lose?'

'Time.' Cynthia was succinct. 'We can't let this matter drag on for weeks.'

'Ask Elaine to talk to her niece.' Martha astonished Cynthia with this agreement. 'She'll come up with nothing. Maybe then we can put this stupidity to rest.'

'There's nothing stupid about this!' Cynthia was incensed. The atmosphere was suddenly charged. 'We don't tolerate Communists in Bentonville.'

'We can gamble a few days on checking her out through Elaine's niece,' Gil soothed. 'And if she comes up with nothing, we'll dig into the emergency fund and hire an investigator. We're not letting this situation continue. Let's meet again on Wednesday evening.' He turned to Cynthia. 'Same time, same place?'

In the Goldberg's cozy dining room the two young couples – Karen and Howie, Laurie and Neil – were deep in earnest discussion.

'If they are having an emergency meeting right now,' Howie plunged in zealously, 'the word will seep out and—'

'Howie, they are having the meeting.' Karen was impatient with him. 'Word leaked through to Neil's mother.'

'A lot of false information "leaks through" in this town,' Howie reminded. 'But if there is a meeting, we'll know. If the Board makes accusations, we'll deal.'

'They mean to fire me.' Laurie struggled for composure. Was Neil right? Should she have waited to see if someone else came forward? *No, I had to do it now.* 'Something horrible is affecting this country. If it can happen here in Bentonville, it can happen anywhere.'

'If they dare to fire you, we'll sue,' Howie promised. 'I'll represent you. We'll demand proof. In this country, you're innocent until proven guilty – beyond a reasonable doubt.'

'But right now,' Neil said, his eyes pained, 'nobody seems to remember that. This country is infected by a terrible disease. It's not just happening in Washington and Hollywood and New York. Now it's reaching its tentacles out to affect other – unexpected – places. It isn't happening just in Bentonville – it's cropping up all over the country.'

'Wouldn't you think Kerensky would fight

back?' Laurie waited for no comment. 'But what chance would he have? What chance will I have if that sanctimonious School Board decides I don't belong in their school?'

'We'll fight.' Howie was grim. 'I can't believe that everybody in this town will accept such a move. I don't care if I lose every client I have – I'll fight this, Laurie.'

'It could be a test case—' Neil seemed to be searching for words. 'But we know what's happening with the HUAC,' he dismissed. 'The Screen Writers' Guild magazine issued a blazing condemnation of the havoc the HUAC was creating in the film business – it meant nothing. They're still wrecking careers.'

'Neil, we can't sit back and do nothing,' Karen protested. 'If – and we don't know that this will happen – the Board fires Laurie, then we must take some kind of action. A lawsuit, like Howie said.'

'We'll be tilting at windmills.' Neil was blunt.

'Suppose a group of teachers approached the Board and fought this—' Karen squinted in thought. 'Neil, you and I can't be the only teachers who'd fight the Board.'

'Want to bet?' Neil challenged. 'They're all scared for their jobs.'

'Nothing's happened yet.' Karen forced a

defiant smile. 'If it does, then Howie will file a lawsuit. We'll fight.'

On Sunday morning – despite the threat of more rain – Laurie walked into town to pick up the Sunday news papers. This morning the friendly news dealer was cold, avoided their usual chit-chat. Ignoring this, Laurie paid for her newspapers and left the shop. She was conscious of a drizzle, glanced up at the sky with trepidation. The drizzle was becoming a downpour. She began to run in the direction of home.

A block further she spied Neil's car approaching. He pulled to a stop at the curb, leaned forward to open the door.

'Get in before you're drenched,' he ordered.

'Oh, what luck you happened along.' She was breathless from running.

Neil chuckled. 'I didn't just happen along. I went to your apartment and saw you weren't there. I figured you'd gone for the papers. Are they dry?'

'Hopefully.' She spread the two Sunday papers across her lap as Neil made a U-turn and headed home. 'Oh!' she gasped, her eyes spanning the headline of the *Record*. 'REDS INVADE BENTONVILLE SCHOOL. LOCALS INDIGNANT.'

Neil's eyes left the road for an instant. 'Damn them! But then we should have expected something like that.' He was struggling to sound philosophical. 'Mom's in a gourmet mood. I'm to bring you back to sample her new recipe for banana fritters. I think she's spiking them with rum.'

'People will begin to think I'm a boarder.' *Am I going to bring grief to Neil and his mother? Guilt by association?*

The three of them – Laurie, Neil, and Beth – settled down to read the Sunday papers after a leisurely breakfast. At intervals Laurie worried about her apartment roof. With this continuous rain would that hint of a leak in her kitchen become serious?

Over lunch Beth reported on the gossip she'd picked up at the book store.

'I hear good things about you, Laurie,' she comforted. 'Your kids love you – and that carries a lot of weight with parents.'

'I have twenty-two students.' Laurie's smile was wry. 'Not even all their parents approve of me. That doesn't give me much leverage.'

'Not everybody believes the craziness in the *Record*,' Beth insisted. 'You're not without friends in this town. I went to The Oasis for a quick lunch, and Sophie Kahn was full of praises for you.'

'Mom, the friends are few.' Neil was somber. He turned to Laurie. 'Maybe you should write another letter to the *Enquirer* –

explaining your side. Make it clear you're not a Commie sympathizer. You could—'

'No more letters,' Laurie broke in. 'I won't grovel.' Her eyes were blazing now. 'I've done nothing wrong.'

Seventeen

Laurie debated calling Tim and Iris to tell them what was happening. No, she rejected this. Why upset them? They'd urge her to come back to New York. But if the Board should fire her, what else was there for her in Bentonville? What future for her and Neil? This was his world.

Tomorrow was a school day – she should go to bed. But she knew sleep would be elusive. All right, get in bed and read a while. She was conscious of rain beating on the roof. Was that wet spot in the kitchen growing worse?

She went into the kitchen, inspected the ceiling. There wasn't just a wet spot now. Rain water dripped from ceiling to floor. She brought out a pot, placed it in a strategic spot. First thing tomorrow morning she must report this to the Kendricks.

She prepared for bed, settled herself with a current copy of the *Saturday Evening Post*. But her mind refused to cooperate. What had happened at that Board meeting last night? So far no word had leaked out. But it would, she told herself grimly.

How could Neil have asked her to write what would amount to a letter of apology to the *Enquirer*? That wasn't what she had expected of him. She felt a disconcerting barrier arising between them despite the way they felt about each other. *What kind of life can we have together if I'm a pariah in this town?*

Eventually she drifted off into troubled slumber, awoke earlier than usual. Reluctant to leave the comfort of her bed just yet, she listened for sounds of rain. No, it was a clear day. Now a thread of sunlight seeped through her bedroom drapes.

All right, get up, face the day. What had happened at that Board meeting Saturday evening? she asked herself for the hundredth time. Would she arrive at school to be told she was fired? Whatever, it must be faced.

She was dawdling over her breakfast when the phone rang. Neil or Karen, she assumed. Nobody else would call at this hour. She hurried to respond.

'Hello—'

'Laurie, it's me. Sharon. Am I calling too early?' she asked apologetically.

'Are you kidding?' Laurie chuckled. 'I'll be heading for school in twenty minutes.' *Why is Sharon calling me?*

'I felt I should tell you. I mean, you should

205

know—' Sharon was stammering in her unease.

'Know what, Sharon?' Laurie pressed, her heart pounding now.

'There was an emergency School Board meeting last evening,' Sharon said. 'To discuss your fitness to teach at the school. They're doing some investigating – I don't know how – and there'll be another meeting on Wednesday evening. I'm not sure I should be telling you this—'

'I'd heard about Saturday's meeting. I didn't know about the one to be held on Wednesday. Thank you for telling me. But I don't know what they expect to unearth about me that could label me unfit to teach here.' *That I served in the WACs?*

'If you're all clear, then there'll be nothing to worry about,' Sharon said with forced optimism. 'At least they're checking before making some rash decision.'

'Yes, that's important.' Laurie tried to mirror Sharon's optimism. The HUAC investigated people – and emerged with horrendous decisions, her mind taunted.

'Laurie, remember – this conversation never happened. I mean, I have to live in this town.'

'It never happened,' Laurie agreed. 'And thanks for calling.'

Off the phone, Laurie tried to deal with what Sharon had told her. She was being 'investigated'. But what could they possibly find to validate firing her? Some clear-thinking souls on the School Board were on her side, she realized with a rush of gratitude. As Neil had said – she wasn't alone.

But she closed her eyes, heard Iris's indignant voice again.

'It kills me when I think of what's happening in this country! The lives that have been ruined! For no good reason – just because somebody suspects that they're on the wrong side of the fence.'

But the School Board didn't jump into a rash decision to fire me. Sane voices prevailed. This battle isn't over.

Laurie left her apartment, circled around to the front of the house, rang the bell. The door opened. Maisie Kendrick stood there.

'Yeah?' A wary glint in her eyes, as though she anticipated trouble.

'There's a leak in my kitchen,' Laurie explained. 'From the roof,' she amplified because Maisie was staring with startling belligerence. 'All that rain, I suppose.'

'I'll have Bud look at it,' Maisie promised, appearing anxious to end the conversation.

'Thanks.' *Why is she looking at me like that? As though trying to make up her mind to say something.* But then Laurie understood. Maisie read the *Record*, had only contempt for the *Enquirer*. *Will she try to evict me from my apartment?*

Her mind in tumult, Laurie headed for school. This was one of the mornings when Neil met with his debating group. She'd walk to school alone. The brief phone conversation with Sharon ticker-taped across her mind as she walked. Sharon was a good person – yet nervous about being regarded as her friend.

Approaching the school entrance she was conscious of a tightness between her shoulderblades, of a knot in her stomach. *But I haven't been fired. I'm just 'under investigation'. What can they possibly learn about me that will give them a reason to fire me?*

She went directly to her classroom – head high, ignoring furtive stares. This was just another day of classes. The School Board would do their 'investigation' – and this insanity would all be over. *It isn't like with Boris Kerensky – they aren't firing me on the basis of ugly rumors. They're investigating – that's a big difference.*

She welcomed the warmth of her students. No reflection from most of them of ugly talk at home. Though darling Betsy Mitchell seemed upset. Talk at the Mitchell household, she interpreted. But this would soon be over, she told herself with fresh optimism. She would be cleared.

Still, at lunch time she was aware that neither Sharon nor Pat appeared in the elementary teachers' lunchroom. Karen shrugged this off with a pithy comment.

'I should be grateful for the investigation,' Laurie said. Karen, too, had heard via the grapevine that 'the new third grade teacher is being investigated'. 'At least the School Board isn't acting on rumors.'

'I don't trust the Board.' Karen radiated skepticism. 'They're just covering their butts. Or, more likely, some members – probably Martha Madison and Jason Smith – put up a fight, so they're making a show of checking you out. Honey, you're not out of the woods yet.'

Bud Kendrick stood at the side of the house – a bottle of beer in hand – and watched while Chuck, his nineteen-year-old sometimes helper, finished repairing the small area of the roof that leaked. Lately he was nervous about climbing on roofs. Chuck was the son of one of his bowling buddies, and with candid reluctance accepted occasional odd jobs. Most of the time Chuck just bitched about how there were 'no real jobs in this dumb town'.

'Hi.' Laurie paused beside Bud, gazed up at the roof. 'Was it a major job?' she asked with a conciliatory smile.

'Nothin' Chuck and me couldn't handle.' He shrugged, covertly inspecting Laurie's slim but curvaceous figure. 'It's almost done.'

'Thanks for taking care of it so fast.' Laurie headed for her front door. She remembered Maisie Kendrick's coldness this morning. Maybe she'd just imagined that. In her apartment she shed her jacket, went into the kitchen to put up a kettle for tea, brought down a cup and a teabag. The pot that sat beneath the leak was half full, but there was no drip coming down from the ceiling now. She'd been leery about the readiness of the Kendricks to take care of repairs. She'd been overly suspicious.

Pouring water into the tea cup, she heard the doorbell. She went to respond. Chuck – the worker she'd seen on the roof – lounged in the doorway.

'Can I come in and check on the ceiling?' he asked, his eyes too bold as they lingered on the high rise of her breasts.

'Sure.' But she pointedly left the front door open despite the chill in the air.

He sauntered into the kitchen, pulled a chair just beneath the wet area in the ceiling, climbed up.

'Yeah, it's okay—' He ran his tongue across his lower lip while he inspected her. 'Good.'

All at once she was uncomfortable. Why doesn't he leave?

'You're new in town—'

'That's right.'

'Bet you don't know many guys yet.' His eyes undressing her.

'I don't consider that a problem,' she shot back.

'If you feel like having fun some night –' he began, but she interrupted.

'No thanks. I'll be otherwise occupied,' she said crisply. What an obnoxious kid!

He turned red, scowled. 'You don't know what you're missin'.' He stalked to the door, slammed it behind him.

'What did you have to pay that young skunk?' Maisie demanded of Bud.

'Not much,' he dodged. 'Look, I ain't climbin' on roofs no more. I'm gettin' too old for that crap.'

'We shoulda let the little bitch drown in the kitchen,' Maisie said savagely. 'You read about her in the *Record*.'

'So? We got no kids in the school.'

'You think maybe with all that stink they're gonna fire her?'

'What's it to us?'

'I don't like livin' with scum,' she bristled, then paused. 'If she gets fired, she won't be able to pay the rent. We need that dough.'

'Nobody's firin' her yet. The apartment stayed empty for over three months before she showed up. Don't go lookin' for trouble.'

'Somebody in this town will fix her

wagon,' Maisie predicted – her smile malicious. She frowned at the sound of the doorbell. 'Who's botherin' us now?'

Chuck had returned. 'I just remembered,' he said, strolling into the foyer. 'You said somethin' about maybe the house needed a paint job. I ain't busy next week—'

'Paint costs money,' Maisie told him before Bud could reply. 'Which is short around here.' She gazed at her husband with contempt.

'Hell, so the house needs a paint job,' Bud said. 'So what? The damn house can burn down for all I care.' He uttered a sardonic laugh. 'We could take the insurance money and move up to Montreal. Maisie's sister lives up there,' he told Chuck. 'Rattlin' around in a big old house all by herself.'

'We're goin' up there tomorrow.' Maisie's face brightened. 'We're stayin' for most of the week. It's my sister's birthday – she gets antsy alone up there in that big house.'

'You change your mind about the paint job,' Chuck flipped, 'I'm available.'

Elaine Jackson's hand tightened on the phone. Her voice was electric. 'Marianne, I was getting anxious at not hearing from you. What have you come up with? The School Board meeting is tomorrow night.'

'I had to do some chasing around, Aunt Elaine.' Marianne was defensive. 'I told you

– I didn't know Laurie Evans personally, though I'd heard about her.' Sarcasm edged her voice. 'She was always active on campus.'

'What did you learn?' Elaine's patience was strained.

'Well, first of all, she speaks three or four languages. When she was growing up, her parents lived all over the world. They were supposed to be in the diplomatic service.' The implication was that Marianne considered this a cover for other activities. 'They're both dead – they died in some mysterious plane crash.'

'Ah-hah!' Elaine felt a surge of triumph. 'Oh, we're on the right track all right!'

'She was involved in all kinds of protest movements on campus – plus she was a WAC.'

'I don't think she mentioned that on her job application—'

'Well, of course, she wouldn't,' Marianne scoffed. 'But wait, there's more. Her brother – and they're very close – fought with the Loyalists in Spain. On the side of the lousy Communists!'

Eighteen

Laurie sat with Karen in the elementary teachers' lunchroom and tried to pretend that all was right with her world. Again, Pat and Sharon had not appeared to share their table.

'Howie says that new diner that opened up isn't bad at all,' Karen said and paused. 'That's where our erstwhile lunch mates are filling their faces these days. Howie saw them there yesterday.'

'The diner will be no competition for The Oasis,' Laurie predicted. It was weird, she thought, how they could sit here and talk so casually. Everybody in this lunchroom – almost everybody in town by now – knew she was being tried in the School Board court. They all knew that her whole future hung in the balance. If she was fired from this school, then who else would hire her?

'Neil tells me his mother is a five star chef.' Karen's tone was gentle. 'I'm looking forward to dinner at his house tomorrow night.'

Beth had arranged another of her last-minute dinners, Laurie understood, to provide some diversion for her tomorrow. The waiting would be almost unbearable. Karen and Howie, Eric, and she made up the dinner guest list. Gail and Joe Simpson had turned down the invitation. They'd mentioned some previous engagement – vague, Beth said. Probably a fabrication. Laurie recalled their discomfort when the subject of the canceled concert had arisen that night at dinner at the Winston house.

'Worst case scenario,' Karen began compassionately, 'Howie will institute a suit. We'll—'

'I don't want to think about that.' Laurie shuddered. 'I keep telling myself, "What can they find out about me that would justify firing me?" I'm not without friends on the School Board, it appears.'

'The word is that Martha Madison and Jason Smith are determined to thwart any rash move.' Karen was somber. 'But that's two out of seven.'

'I'm not going to think about it,' Laurie lied. 'We're going to have a lovely dinner party tomorrow night. I won't let anything spoil that.'

As Laurie had expected, she found Neil waiting for her at the entrance at the end of the school day.

'Hi—' He smiled with devastating warmth

at the sight of her. He was determined to let everybody in the school know that he was on her side – even though he'd disapproved of her sending the letter to the *Enquirer*.

'The rain's over for sure.' She returned his smile. 'And my kitchen leak was fixed.' If they were fifteen years younger, she thought with a rush of tenderness, he'd offer to carry her tote.

'The Kendricks wouldn't win any prize as landlords.' He grimaced in distaste. 'I remember the last couple who lived in the apartment complained that nothing was ever fixed before a dozen pleas.'

'This time they were protecting their property.' Laurie shrugged. 'It wasn't for love of me.' She remembered Maisie Kendrick's scathing attitude when she'd gone to report the leak. 'They left early this morning for Montreal, I gather.'

Neil exchanged pleasantries with a pair of teachers crossing to the parking area. Laurie noted how they avoided eye contact with her.

'I wish I could go into that School Board meeting tomorrow evening and tell them how crazy they're acting,' Neil whispered and reached for her arm as they took a short cut towards their destination. 'But of course they'd never believe me. They all knew I'm "mad about the girl".'

'And I'm "mad about the boy",' she

216

murmured.

'Laurie—' He took a deep breath. 'Why don't we announce our engagement? We can wait for the wedding until you're ready – but let people know how we feel about each other.'

Laughter lit her face. 'I suspect they know.' Now she was serious. 'But this isn't the time for an official announcement.'

If she was fired, there could be nothing for Neil and her. Face it. She couldn't stay in this town if that happened – and it would be horribly unfair to take Neil from the only world he'd ever known. He had a great future here. Everybody expected him to move into politics, to take an active role in running Bentonville. He'd come to hate her if she deprived him of that.

Laurie knew when she awoke Wednesday morning that this would be an intolerable day. She was determined to go through it with her head held high. The whole town knew, she thought for the hundredth time, that she was being tried this evening. They even knew the time when the meeting would commence.

Karen had insisted they go out to lunch today. 'Howie says this is the day The Oasis has their roast beef special. Let's live it up.'

Laurie ate lunch without tasting. When they paid their checks, she talked with

Sophie Kahn about little David, who was the favorite of all her students – though, of course, she gave no inkling of this to the class. Sophie glowed. What a delightful woman, Laurie thought. Her awful wartime experiences hadn't destroyed her zest for living. Or was that motivated by her love for David? Always sadness seemed to lurk in her eyes.

'We'd better get moving,' Karen said. 'We're running short on time.'

Returning to her classroom, Laurie calculated that in exactly four hours her fate in this town would be sealed. And there was nothing she could do that would affect the decision.

Cynthia Andrews sat – stiff and triumphant – at the head of the conference table in her den while Ted Jackson wound up his report on Laurie Evans.

'Elaine's niece is a real bird dog,' Ted said with satisfaction. 'She even managed to check on books Evans took out at the library while she was a student at Columbia.' He paused for dramatic effect. 'Karl Marx, Engels, Clifford Odets – who wrote those Commie plays. She may not be showing off a membership card, but it's clear enough where her sympathies lie. Her brother fought with the Loyalists in Spain. She's here to spread the same word.'

'I vote we discharge her,' Gil Taylor said brusquely with a glance at his watch.

'I haven't heard anything that warrants that action.' Martha Madison's calm voice was belied by the fire in her eyes. 'So she read Karl Marx, Engels, Clifford Odets in college. So did I. For a school paper. No doubt she did the same.'

Cynthia stared with ill-concealed rage at Martha. What was the matter with that woman? How had she ever managed to get on the School Board? Wherever she showed up, she was trouble.

'Does anybody else wish to make a statement about this teacher?' Cynthia's gaze swept about the table.

'I must admit I'm not sure she's guilty of anything,' a heretofore silent member contributed. 'But we can't afford to gamble with the minds of our youngsters. Rather one teacher hurt than a whole classroom of children.'

'Then let's take a vote,' Cynthia said. Make this a short meeting. Ralph liked an early dinner. He could be so grumpy if it was delayed.

'Not just yet,' Jason demurred. 'I haven't heard a word that tells me Evans is a Communist.'

'Are you kidding?' Gil was exasperated. 'Non-Communists don't get hysterical when a concert is canceled in their town.

219

They take it for granted that the committee that did the canceling had good and sufficient reason. They—'

'But the committee didn't have a reason,' Martha objected. 'It was a stupid witch-hunt.'

'Come on, Martha,' Gil scoffed. 'That man Kerensky signed all kinds of petitions. He—'

'You saw those petitions?' Martha challenged.

'Respected people reported on them.' Gil sighed with strained patience. 'The man has been canceled in half a dozen cities. Where there's smoke, there's fire. Like with the Evans woman. Why would she have gotten so excited about the cancellation if she wasn't a Red herself?'

'I was excited – upset – about the cancellation.' Martha leaned forward in challenge. 'Does that make me a Communist?'

'You're a misguided woman,' Gil dodged. His smile was supercilious. 'God knows, we see that often enough.' He turned to Cynthia. 'Let's take a vote. I want to go to sleep tonight with a good conscience.'

With a tight smile Cynthia asked each member of the Board to vote. No doubt in her mind about the outcome. Only two members voted to retain Laurie Evans as a teacher in the Bentonville school system.

'Then let's draft the discharge notice,'

Cynthia said briskly. 'It'll be delivered officially to Carl Franklin before classes begin
tomorrow morning. I'll phone him tonight
so he can arrange for a last-minute substitute teacher to be on hand to take
Evans' class.'

'This is the kind of action that makes me
ashamed of being a member of the School
Board.' Martha's eyes swept about the table.
'I never expected to feel such disgust for
fellow Board members.'

'That's uncalled for!' Cynthia gazed at
Martha in fury. How dare she talk that way!

'Here's something else that's uncalled for.'
Martha rose to her feet. 'My resignation.'

Nineteen

The atmosphere in the Winston dining room seemed almost convivial. Almost.

'Beth, this roast is superb,' Eric said. 'Nobody in this town cooks like you.'

'A roast is easy,' Beth confided. 'You throw it in the oven and forget about it.'

'You have a special throw.' Laurie tried to contribute to the convivial mood. But she was ever conscious that at this moment the School Board was probably concluding its meeting. What was their decision? *My whole life is hanging in the balance. Not just the job. My life.*

'Beth, you're to cooking what Bob Feller is to baseball,' Eric declared. 'Keep pitching.'

Now Howie talked about the Joe Louis-Ezzard Charles fight at Yankee Stadium. 'I hated like hell seeing Joe Louis lose,' he said plaintively. 'Hell, the sportswriters are calling him old at thirty-six.' He chuckled. 'I'm close enough to resent it.'

'You're a baby,' Beth scolded. 'You've got your best years ahead of you.'

Laurie stared down at her plate. *What do I*

have ahead of me? It all depends on what happened at the Board meeting. First Tim, then Neil warned me against impulsive actions. But I was right! The Arts League Committee committed an unpardonable sin in canceling the Kerensky concert.

Without meaning to inflict a morbid note, Karen introduced the subject of the Korean 'police action'.

'It's war,' she said, and winced. 'Soldiers are dying on both sides. Nehru is right when he warns that by invading North Korea we could bring Communist China and even Russia into the war.' She stopped short with an air of apology. This was not a moment to talk about Communism. 'Has anybody seen *The Breaking Point*? I hear it's great. Though I didn't care for the novel. I may be going against popular opinion, but Hemingway isn't my favorite novelist.'

Laurie tensed, hurtling back through the years. She remembered when Tim returned from Spain and talked about Hemingway.

'Hemingway held court in the lobby of the Florida Hotel in Madrid. He was in Spain, he said, to fight fascism. Sure, at one point he coached International Brigade recruits on handling weapons and even made visits to the line – not always appreciated. On one occasion, at least, the results were unfortunate – but he didn't hang around to watch.'

In some crazy way, Laurie warned herself

with sudden prescience, the School Board might learn – in their 'investigation' – that her brother had fought with the Loyalists in Spain. But they wouldn't learn – would they? – about his total disillusionment with that war.

Because this was a midweek night it was accepted that the dinner party would conclude at an early hour. Yet the air was full of unease. Close to ten o'clock – with everyone conscious of the hour – Beth brought up the subject that tugged at everyone's mind.

'The School Board meeting was probably over hours ago.' Beth was choosing her words with care. 'Do you suppose there's someone we could call to ferret out information?' Her eyes swept about in hope.

'It's late to make a call,' Karen said uncertainly, her gaze focused on Laurie. 'But under the circumstances—' Her voice trailed off.

Howie cleared his throat. 'I've worked with Martha Madison on several projects. Maybe I could give her a buzz.'

'Do it,' Beth urged.

Laurie's heart pounded while Howie crossed to the telephone. Martha Madison was a friend, yes – but as the others said, she had only two friends on the School Board. Could they have prevailed?

'Martha, I apologize for calling so late in

the evening,' Howie said when she responded, 'but you must know that Laurie Evans is enduring a rough evening.' He paused. 'That's right,' he conceded. 'We're anxious to know the outcome of the Board meeting.' He sighed. 'Sure, most of the town knows about tonight's meeting.' Again, a pause while he listened to what Martha had to say at the other end. 'I understand – and thanks, Martha.' His face tense, he put down the phone.

'Well?' Beth demanded.

'Martha reminded me that, of course, she wasn't free to announce the Board's verdict.' He took a deep breath. 'But she did tell me that – as a result of the vote – she's resigned as a member of the School Board.'

Laurie alone of the dinner party guests remained at the Winston house. So it was all over, she told herself with a blend of rage and numbness. She was being fired from her very first job as a teacher.

'Laurie, would you like to spend the night here?' Beth asked solicitously. 'We have a guest room.'

Laurie managed a wan smile. 'Thank you, but no. I'll go home. I – I need to think some things out.'

'I'll walk you home,' Neil said.

A sharp wind had come up in the course of the evening. Tomorrow, Laurie thought abstractedly, the ground would be covered with leaves. As they walked, Neil clung to her hand. She knew that he would come into the apartment with her. She wanted those few private moments with him.

'You don't have to go to school tomorrow,' he said tentatively, pulling her close.

'I'll go,' she said after a moment. *How can this be happening? I'm nobody. Tim said it only happened to well-known people. Actors and writers and musicians.*

'I'm going to see Jim Peters before class,' Neil decided. 'He's always at his desk by seven a.m. We're going to fight this, Laurie. And you heard Howie – as soon as the School Board's decision is announced officially, he's going to file a civil suit.'

'Was I so wrong in what I said in my letter?' Her eyes searched his.

'You were right, and you were courage-ous.'

They clung together in passion born of love. Neil was the one man in the world with whom she wished to spend her life – and she had deprived herself of this.

'I love you. I think you're the bravest woman I've ever known,' he whispered, his mouth at her ear. 'And I'd better leave this minute before I take advantage of you in a bad moment.' His eyes were tenderly teas-ing.

'You won't be afraid to walk with me to

school tomorrow morning?' she jibed with an effort at humor. 'You know, guilt by association?'

'Come over for breakfast,' he ordered. 'We'll walk to school together.'

Laurie stood at a window and watched Neil disappear from view. Life would never be the same after tomorrow morning. Would she be stopped at the door by Mr Franklin and given her walking papers? She closed her eyes in anguish as she visualized the shock her class would receive. *They love me. They do!*

Now Laurie began the routine preparations for bed. From habit she crossed to open a window. It refused to budge. She tried the other window. Nothing happened. So the windows were stuck. She'd worry about that tomorrow.

Even though both bedroom windows were closed, she was conscious of a sharp chill in the room. She was glad for the warmth of her flannel nightie. She reached for a magazine and slid beneath the covers, reached to flip on the bedside radio.

The raucous sounds of *Jukebox Saturday Night* poured into the room. Laurie froze. Her bedside radio was set to the local station that played only classical music between 8 p.m. and 11 p.m. *Someone's been in the apartment.* Enclosed in eerie alarm, she tossed aside the covers, slid her feet into slippers beside the bed and began a minute search for further evidence.

Her mind argued that the station had made other arrangements, that the absence of classical music meant nothing. Fighting a touch of panic she sought out the day's *Enquirer*, with trembling hands turned to the radio listings. No change. The station had scheduled three hours of classical music. As usual. Someone had come into the apartment, moved the radio dial.

Now her eyes focused on the low, narrow bookcase against one living-room wall, clung to the unoccupied spot on one bookshelf. There were normally no empty spaces, her mind pinpointed. She glanced around the room. A book lay on the club chair. A book she hadn't read in months. Somebody had come into this apartment, had lain on her bed and listened to music. Someone had taken that book from the bookcase, sat in that chair, read for a moment, then discarded the book.

Who had come into the apartment? Why?

All right, she ordered herself – discuss this tomorrow morning with Neil. For now go back into the bedroom – where some stranger had lain on her bed – and try to sleep.

She forced herself to switch off the lamp. She lay tense and fearful in the blackness of the night. Outdoors the wind wailed as though in torment. For what seemed like hours she tossed from one side of the bed to the other – futilely courting sleep. At last – from exhaustion – she drifted into troubled slumber.

With subconscious reluctance – without opening her eyes – she awakened. An odd stench assailed her nostrils. Strange sounds filled the room. All at once she was fully conscious. Her eyes fluttered open. Towering orange-red flames engulfed the living room, were surging into the bedroom. Already approaching her bed.

She sprang from the far side of the bed, darted to a window, tugged. But both windows had been stuck when she'd tried to open them earlier. A window was the only means of escape. Fighting panic, she reached for a chair, smashed one window, climbed onto the chair. Disregarding jagged glass in her haste, she wriggled through the window, managed to drop to the earth below.

Struggling for breath, she paused a moment, then ran – barefoot, clad only in her flannel nightgown – through the dark night to the house across the street. In the smell that had awoken her, the aroma of gasoline had mingled with the smoke. Somebody had meant to kill her. The somebody who had sneaked into her apartment while she was having dinner across the way – to plot this attempt at murder.

Distraught, terrified, she leaned on the bell of the Winston house. She saw lights go on in two rooms, waited for Neil or his mother to respond.

The door swung wide. For an instant Neil gaped in shock. He drew her within the house. His eyes fastened on the rapidly developing fire across the street. The wind a demon that drove it forward.

'Somebody meant to kill me,' she gasped. 'I smelled gasoline. The fire was arson!'

Twenty

'Your arm is bleeding.' Beth's eyes were drawn to a gash on Laurie's right arm.

'Take care of her, Mom,' Neil ordered. 'I'll call the fire department.' He charged towards the living-room phone.

'I don't know,' Beth faltered. 'Perhaps we ought to take you to the hospital Emergency Room—'

'No!' Laurie and Neil exclaimed simultaneously.

'It's not a deep cut,' Laurie said shakily. 'I had to break the window glass to get out of the apartment.'

As Beth led her to the bathroom and medical supplies, Laurie heard Neil's terse report of the fire. Moments later they heard the shrill siren that summoned volunteer firemen to the fire house.

Neil appeared in the doorway. The siren continued to shriek. 'The gusts are terrific,' he reported uneasily, frowning in thought. 'The way the flames are engulfing the house I doubt there'll be anything left but ashes. Laurie, until we know who's responsible,

231

you must remain out of sight.'

Laurie felt encased in ice. 'You mean, whoever set the fire may try again.'

'That's right.' Neil turned to stare out a window. 'Let everyone believe you died in the fire. Until—'

'But they'll expect to find some remains,' Beth broke in – and winced.

'That fire was set to burn the house down to the ground,' Neil reminded. 'Sure, they'll search. But they'll find nothing. But meanwhile we must – somehow – track down whoever saturated the house with gasoline and sealed the bedroom windows. It was premeditated murder. Thank God, Laurie, you awoke in time to escape.'

'Another two minutes and it would have been too late.' Laurie shivered in recall.

'To make sure he – or she – doesn't try again, you must stay hidden here in the house. Nobody will know you're here,' Beth comforted. 'We'll find whoever started the fire.'

'Yes,' Laurie whispered in agreement.

'Let's go to my bedroom,' Beth prodded. 'I'll find a robe for you.'

Only now did Laurie realize she stood here barefoot, clad only in her flannel nightgown. *This is a nightmare. How could this have happened? Who hated me enough to try to kill me?*

'I'd better dash out and show myself,' Neil

said. 'Mom, wait a few minutes, then put in an appearance at the door. Nobody must suspect Laurie is here.'

The shriek of speeding fire trucks penetrated the night quiet. In moments they would be pulling up before the house. Neil turned up the collar of his plaid wool bathrobe and strode out into the night. He saw lights flashing on in surrounding houses. The Kendricks' next-door neighbors rushed out of their house.

Flames wrapped around the wing of the house that had been Laurie's apartment with a menacing grip, soared to startling heights. Neil raced as close to the blaze as was prudent. He must make a show of believing Laurie was inside.

The couple who lived next door, along with their teenaged daughters, hurried to the scene, flinched at the heat that greeted them. The fire truck drew to a stop. Firemen leaped to the ground.

'What's that smell?' the man from the next house asked Neil.

'Gasoline,' Neil told him. 'The fire was set.'

A few moments later a fireman who'd approached backed away. 'No way can we get into the house!' He turned to Neil – just as the second fire truck screeched to a stop. 'Anybody inside?'

'Yes!' Neil was terse. 'Our new third grade

teacher!'

'The Kendricks are up in Montreal,' another neighbor – just arriving on the scene – contributed. 'They left Monday morning – they won't be back until Sunday night.'

The police chief arrived, raced to consult with the firemen.

'All we can do is try to stop it from spreading,' one of the men told the police chief. 'We can't go in. The flames are too huge, too hot.'

'It's arson, Ted,' Neil called to the police chief. His anguish obvious. 'Somebody meant to kill Laurie Evans—' He gestured his shock and grief.

Neighbors huddled close by. One young mother, holding a toddler in the bitter cold, sobbed.

'She didn't have a chance! How could it have spread so fast?' another cried in frustration.

Neil was aware of covert glances of sympathy in his direction. They all knew how he felt about Laurie. But earlier tonight, he thought in inner rage – because of the horrendous gossip that spread through this town like a plague – the School Board had voted to fire Laurie.

All at once a plot took root in his mind. By tomorrow morning all of Bentonville would believe that Laurie had died in a fire set by an arsonist. An arsonist driven to this by the witch-hunting that had engulfed the town. Let him take up the battle that Laurie had begun. Let him join with her to make this town understand what it had done. This town must go on trial.

With an air of reluctance the neighbors who had emerged at the sound of the fire trucks began to return to their houses. A sense of shock, of tragedy unexpected hung over them. Only Neil remained. One fire truck packed up to leave. A fireman approached Neil, hesitated before he spoke. His eyes bright with compassion.

'There was nothing we could do – it spread too fast, too hot.'

'I know,' Neil acknowledged.

He remained – a solitary figure on the perimeter of activities. Shaking from the unseasonable cold but determined to wait.

'Why don't you go on home?' another fireman suggested solicitously. 'We'll have to hang around for hours – to make sure the embers don't start up again. Go home, Neil. There's nothing you can do here.'

In the guest room – with Neil at her side – Laurie sipped at the hot tea Beth had brought her. Everything that had happened in the past three hours seemed unreal. Two firemen remained at what was left of the Kendrick house.

'I've never seen a fire here in town that

was so devastating.' Beth shuddered as she joined Laurie and Neil.

'Everything's gone.' Laurie shook her head in disbelief. 'Everything.' But in a corner of her mind she recalled with gratitude that she had left a large carton of personal mementos – photographs of her parents, Tim and herself as children, other such items – in Tim and Iris's apartment until she had acquired larger quarters. 'I don't have a thing to wear—'

'Spoken like a woman,' Neil jibed gently.

'I suppose we ought to try to get a little sleep,' Beth said, doubt in her voice that this was possible tonight. 'It's almost five a.m.'

In three and a half hours classes would begin, Laurie thought. But she wouldn't be going to teach today. Even if there'd been no fire, she wouldn't be teaching. The School Board would have seen to that.

'The radio station starts its day at 5 a.m.,' Neil said. 'News of the fire will spread quickly.' He paused. 'I suspect the police chief will report it as suspicious.'

'Suspicious?' Beth exploded. 'Everybody out there last night must have smelled the gasoline. It was arson!'

'The newspapers will report that you died in the fire,' Neil told Laurie. 'There'll be nothing left to identify. And let this town face its crime.' His face was taut. 'I'll go to the *Enquirer* on my lunch hour, talk to Jim

Peters. I'll demand we hold a town meeting tomorrow afternoon. We'll—'

'I have to call Tim and tell him what's happened,' Laurie said in sudden alarm. 'I can't let him believe I died in the fire! He'd be terrified if he tried to phone and was told the line was no longer in use.'

'No phone calls,' Neil warned. 'We can't take chances that you'll be heard. We—'

'I'll drive over to the mall near Albany,' Beth offered. 'I can call from there. I'll do some shopping. It'll appear normal.'

Laurie's eyes swept to Neil. He nodded in agreement.

'Give Mom your brother's number. What time does he leave for his office?'

It was arranged for Beth to drive to the mall, to phone Tim early enough to find him at his apartment. She would explain the situation, reassure him. Knowing her, Laurie thought, he wouldn't be totally surprised that she'd landed herself in such tumult.

'All right, to bed now for a couple of hours of sleep.' Beth was firm. 'But set your alarm, Neil. Wake me.' She turned to Laurie. 'To be safe, stay in the guest room with the shades drawn at all times. When I return from the mall, I'll make breakfast and bring it to you. And we'll figure out wardrobe then,' she said with an effort at humor. 'Luckily I'm a pack rat – I have a bunch of clothes I haven't been able to get into for a dozen years. You know, wishful thinking.' She sighed, a glint in her eye. 'But they'll be a reasonable fit for you.'

Tears welled in Laurie's eyes when Beth tucked her in and exhorted her not to worry.

'You did a good thing, Laurie,' Beth insisted. 'It was meant to be. And you know what?' She chuckled. 'I'll bet Bud and Maisie Kendrick will be thrilled when they learn their house burned down. All that insurance money. Lucky for them they were up in Montreal. People might have been suspicious.'

But the Kendrick house wasn't burned down for insurance money. It was meant to kill her.

Twenty-one

The morning was gray and chilly. Beth's initial thought as she came awake – at the normal hour, as though their world had not turned upside down in the course of the night – was to turn up the thermostat. She relished the warmth provided by an efficient furnace.

Her face tightened as memory returned. All right, she told herself grimly, get this show on the road. She meant to be at the shopping mall shortly after 8 a.m. – before Laurie's brother left for his office.

She reached for her robe, headed for the hall to raise the thermostat, heard sounds in the kitchen, sniffed the aroma of coffee perking. Neil was up already. Had he been asleep at all?

'You didn't sleep,' she accused, her eyes tender as they rested on her son.

'It was futile to try,' he admitted. 'Coffee's almost ready.'

'Give me a couple of minutes to throw on some clothes. I'll skip my morning shower, have it later.' She paused in thought. 'I don't

239

think you should go in to school this morning.'

'I haven't missed a day since I had the flu three years ago.' But his eyes told her he understood why she'd said this. 'You're right,' he said after a moment. 'I'll call Franklin right away. That's two substitutes he'll need today.'

When Beth returned to the kitchen, she found Neil on the kitchen extension. He frowned in exasperation.

'I'm sorry, Mr Franklin, there's no way I can hold my classes today. Laurie and I were engaged.' That'll float around town fast, Beth told herself. 'I owe her this respect,' Neil continued. He paused, listening to Franklin – his face expressing impatience. 'Yes, I'll take my classes tomorrow.' He put down the phone. 'The unfeeling bastard!'

'You've never liked him,' Beth reminded. 'Did you expect that to change now?'

'Laurie's still asleep?' he asked.

Unexpectedly Beth smiled. 'I expect she'll sleep for a while. I slipped a pill into her tea. She needs sleep after all that's happened.'

'I'm going over to the *Enquirer* office in a little while.' Neil reached for the percolator, poured coffee for the two of them. 'I have to persuade Jim that I'm right in demanding a town meeting be held tomorrow evening. According to the town laws any citizen can do that. It'll be most efficient if somebody like Jim Peters calls for it.'

Beth was ambivalent. 'How do we know people will come?'

'We'll get on the phone. We'll make sure they come. Maybe Jim can be persuaded to bring out an "extra" this morning. Just one sheet, perhaps – reporting what happened last night. Laying the blame where it belongs – on the people of this town.'

The phone was a jarring intrusion. Beth reached to respond – eyebrows lifted. A phone call at 6:40 a.m.? 'Hello.'

'Beth, you must know about the fire!' a familiar, agitated voice demanded. Gail Simpson. 'I mean, being right across the way from you. Is it true that the firemen couldn't rescue that new teacher?'

'They couldn't,' Beth agreed, remembering Gail's attitude the last time she was a dinner guest in their house.

'It's so sad,' Gail mourned. 'She was so young.'

'We're very unhappy,' Beth said. 'There'll probably be a town meeting,' she added, her eyes meeting Neil's.

'Why?' A wariness in Gail's voice now.

'Because we're responsible. All the gossip about her being a Commie – when she wasn't at all. Everybody knows the School Board was considering firing her. All the nasty talk got through to some crazy character who believed that talk and took vicious action. It was arson, you know.'

'I gather it was suspicious. But she brought it on herself,' Gail said. 'Defending that Commie musician the way she did.'

'Gail, we don't know that he's a Commie. Linwood acted on some silly rumors.'

'But there were other cancellations, too. That's what I heard.'

'That's the trouble that seems to be sweeping this whole country – even nice little towns like Linwood and Bentonville. People believe unsubstantiated rumors – and keep adding to them. It was only Linwood that canceled.'

'Oh, uh, I have to go now. Joe's ready for breakfast.' In self-conscious haste Gail concluded the conversation. 'He has to be in the office early this morning.'

'I'll talk to you soon, Gail.' Beth's face was stormy as she put down the phone. 'Sit down, Neil. Let's have breakfast. Something tells me we'll need it this morning.'

The phone was a raucous intrusion in the bedroom of Cliff Rogers, editor of the *Record*. He frowned, eyes still closed, tugged the blanket over his head. The phone continued to ring. He pulled himself into a semi-sitting position, still reluctant to reply.

'Answer the damn thing,' his wife grunted.

His eyes focused on the clock on the night table. 'Shit.' He picked up the receiver.

'Hello.'

'Cliff, have I got a story for you.' The voice of his brother-in-law Gil Taylor came to him – with indecent alertness considering the hour, he thought.

'Yeah?' He was long bored with Gil's secret yearnings to be an investigative reporter. 'So what's it this time?'

'The School Board met last night.' Importance in his voice.

'So?' For that Gil had to wake him up?

'We got the goods on that new teacher. You know what people have been saying. Well, it's all true. She was into all kinds of Red activities on her college campus. And get this. Before she went to college – on the GI Bill, which taxpayers like you and me pay for – she was a WAC. Plus—' He paused in triumph. 'Her brother fought with the Loyalists – the Commies,' he emphasized, 'in Spain.'

'You coulda told me that an hour later,' Cliff grumbled.

'You didn't hear about the fire yet, did you? She lived in an apartment in the old Kendrick house. Last night somebody torched it. She never got out.'

All at once Cliff was wide awake. 'And now,' he surmised, 'they're going to try to make her a martyr. Whitewash the bitch,' he said with contempt.

'Does this warrant an extra?'

'You bet it does.' Cliff was fully awake now. 'Some folks in this stupid town will try to clean up her act – and blame good citizens like you and me. Within three hours,' he vowed, 'the *Record* will have an extra on the street. Complete with all the juicy details our sharp School Board dug up.'

Neil approached the door to the *Enquirer*'s office with grim determination. The reception room was deserted. The receptionist not due in for another hour, at least, Neil surmised. *All right, I know the direction to Jim's office. Go there.*

Jim Peters looked up with momentary astonishment when Neil appeared in his doorway.

'Yeah, I kind of expected to see you this morning.' He managed a rueful grin. 'Though maybe not this early.'

'You know about the fire? About Laurie Evans?'

'I know. Sit down, Neil.' Jim was somber now. 'A terrible tragedy that never should have happened.'

'I'm here for two reasons.' Neil sat in the chair across from Jim. 'One, I hope you'll have an extra on the streets this morning – in addition to your regular edition. And—'

'It'll be out in less than an hour.' Jim's face reflected his inner anguish. He was blaming himself for this fire, Neil surmised. For publishing Laurie's letter. Only now was Neil aware of the sounds from the rear of the building that told him an extra was in work. 'My spies tell me that the *Record* has an extra about to be distributed as we speak.' He leaned forward, his eyes searching Neil's. 'What was the other thing you wanted to discuss?'

'This town has disgraced itself. I demand it stand trial.'

Jim gaped in doubt. 'Neil, you can't try a town—'

'This time it has to be done. Don't you understand that? I'm making the charge. I'm accusing this town of witch-hunting.'

'That much is true,' Jim conceded. 'But—'

'We've got to make people here realize what they've done,' Neil said urgently. 'Not just to Laurie – to themselves. They've lost sight of the American way of life, turned their backs on all the things our ancestors fought and died to preserve. We must—'

'We'll hold a trial,' Jim broke in with a surge of determination. 'Right on the front pages of the *Enquirer*. I promise you that!'

'That's not enough,' Neil rejected. 'I want to call a town meeting for tomorrow night. That will be our trial.' He took a deep breath. 'We have a right to do that, haven't we?' It was a ruling that existed on the Bentonville books, though he didn't recalled its ever being used.

'Yes, we have that right. But it's awfully short notice.'

'It has to be fast,' Neil insisted. 'Before people start to build up alibis for themselves. If you and the *Enquirer* launch it, we can hold the meeting tomorrow evening. In the school gym,' he specified. 'You have contacts to set that up fast.'

'Yeah, I can do that—' But Jim seemed uneasy.

'Jim, we have to do this! In 1692 American colonists executed nineteen people accused of being witches. In 1950 witch-hunting shouldn't exist in Bentonville, New York.'

'Hmm.' Jim grunted. Neil sensed the wheels turning in his head. 'We'll need somebody important to preside.' Jim was brisk. 'Somebody who carries a lot of weight. That way,' he said with a canny smile, 'they come out of curiosity, if nothing else. But remember,' he warned, 'the gym can hold a total of three hundred people. That's not a hell of a lot—'

'I'll arrange for loudspeakers to carry the proceedings outside,' Neil plotted, churning with a need for action. 'If we can believe the weather man, the rain is over. Tomorrow will be fair and warmer. And what happens at that meeting will spread like a hurricane.'

Jim snapped his fingers. 'Judge Coburn!' he said. 'People respect him. He's fought for good things for Bentonville. He won't turn us down.' He checked his watch. 'I'll call him in about an hour. Meanwhile, I've got an extra to get out on the streets. And a last-minute addition. An emergency town meeting in the high school gym tomorrow night at eight p.m.' He hesitated. 'I can't tell you how much this has shaken me up. That girl was a breath of fresh air in this town.'

Beth fished in her coin purse for change. She wasn't sure what the charge was for a call to New York City. She spread coins across the shelf beneath the pay phone, supplied the amount the telephone operator instructed.

'Hello,' an unfamiliar masculine voice replied.

'Is this Tim Evans?' she asked, with an effort to sound cheerful, lest he be anxious.

'Yes.' Wariness blended with curiosity.

'I'm Beth Winston in Bentonville. Laurie's fine,' she reassured him, 'but she asked me to call you.' As succinctly as possible she briefed Tim on the happenings.

He groaned. 'Leave it to Laurie to get involved in something like that.'

'She was right in what she did,' Beth said swiftly. 'As we're right in trying to make this town understand what they almost did. But Laurie was concerned that if you tried to reach her and couldn't, you'd be alarmed.'

'I'll be in Bentonville some time tomorrow. In time to be present at your town meeting. I'll have something to say, I assure you.'

Jim Peters swigged down the last of his coffee, debated calling Judge Coburn. Hell, Alec was an early riser like himself. Give the old boy a buzz right now. As he reached for the phone, his longtime secretary hurried into the room.

'We're rolling,' Helen announced in triumph and handed him the one-page extra. 'Fresh off the press. The boys are lined up to hit the streets.'

'This is a three-cup coffee morning.' He handed her his empty cup. 'Fill her up.'

Now he dialed Alec Coburn's private number. *My wife's forever on the phone – I need my own line.*

'Hello?' Judge Coburn's mellow voice came over the line.

'Things are hopping around this town,' Jim said with no preliminaries. 'In case you haven't noticed.'

'That statement and the hour of this call tell me you've got a favor to ask,' Coburn grumbled, but it was a familiar routine.

'You've been hearing all the crap about the Arts League's canceling the first concert of the season, I suppose.'

'I've heard some noise,' Coburn conceded. 'Since when were you a patron of the arts?'

'You've heard why it was canceled—'

'Some nonsense about the man's politics,' Coburn drawled.

'Witch-hunting has hit good old Benton-ville. And that's rotten. I gather you've heard about the fire?'

'I heard the damn siren at way past two in the morning. I don't listen to the news until I've had breakfast.'

'You'll be hearing plenty about it,' Jim warned. 'The Kendrick house – you know that creepy couple – well, the house burned down to the ground. It was arson – I hear you could smell the gasoline a block away. But what was so rotten about it' – anger laced his voice now – 'a bright young woman – the school's new third grade teacher – died in the fire.'

'Oh, Lord!'

'Neil Winston – the word is that he was engaged to her – is demanding a town meet-ing. He thinks the town needs to recognize that it's responsible for her death.'

'Jim, you're running ahead of me – I don't get the connection.'

'All this witch-hunting – about her being a Commie. No grounds for it, Alec. All damn supposition. The School Board was about to fire her, for God's sake. Some crazy got hot under the collar and decided to do away with her. We want you to preside at the town meeting. Tomorrow night at eight p.m., in the school gym.'

'Do I have a say in this?' Coburn challenged, a hint of a chuckle in his voice.

'Nope,' Jim told him. 'What's a good time for me to drop around today and fill you in?'

Twenty-two

Slowly Laurie emerged from slumber. She was conscious of a hammering at the back of her head, an unfamiliar stiffness. She frowned in reproach, opened her eyes. Shock waves enveloped her. She was in a strange bed. A strange room.

She sat upright. Her mind a kaleidoscope of nightmarish recall. Her heart pounded. She gazed at her bandaged arm and shivered. How close she had come to dying in that fire!

She aborted an instinct to run to a window to see what remained of the house. Neil said she must remain in hiding until the arsonist was found. But how long would that be? Suppose it never happened?

Her gaze settled on a neat pile of clothes on the chair beside the bed. Beth said she'd put out clothes that might fit. Two pairs of shoes sat on the floor. Neil said that for now her world must consist of the guest bedroom and the bathroom. She wasn't to stir beyond that area. They were to take no chances on the arsonist making another attempt at murder.

The quietness of the house told her she was alone. Beth had gone to phone Tim from the shopping mall, she reminded herself. Had Neil gone to take his classes? She glanced about for a clock, saw the one on the night table beside her bed. It was almost 10 a.m., she realized with astonishment. She'd slept for five hours.

Beth would be at the book shop. Neil at school. She winced, visualizing the shock of her class when a substitute walked into the classroom. Would they be told she'd died in the fire? *Oh, I hope not.* No, she comforted herself – the class wouldn't be given such a brutal report. They'd wait – thank God – for parents to handle the situation. *But how long before I can come out and show myself?*

She was conscious of a sudden need for activity. She left the bed, checked through the pile of clothes, chose what she would need for the day. She slid one foot into a shoe. Too tight. She tried the second pair. Not the greatest fit but they would do.

With clothes in tow she hurried into the bathroom, smiled when she realized Beth had put out fresh towels, a wash cloth, and a toothbrush for her. How would she survive without Beth and Neil?

Under the welcoming hot spray of the shower she forced herself to face reality. What future could there ever be for Neil

and her? Neil had spent his entire life –
except for the war years – here in Bentonville. Everyone expected him to be a leader
– probably mayor – in the not too distant
future. She'd be a liability for him. People
would never forget this ugly period. Why did
it have to be this way, when she and Neil
could be so happy together?

Out of the shower – mindful of Neil's
exhortations – she returned to the guest
room. He was probably at school now, she
thought – and stiffened to attention. She
heard someone come into the house, head
back towards the kitchen.

'Neil?' she said softly, then slightly louder.
'Neil?'

Neil strode into view. 'You must be starving. I'll bring you breakfast in a few minutes. How's your arm?'

'It's fine.' She managed a smile.

He hesitated a moment, pulled newspaper
pages from his jacket. 'You'll want to see
these. An extra put out by the *Enquirer* and
another by the *Record*. We'll have our trial –
our town meeting,' he revised, 'tomorrow
evening at eight p.m. Jim Peters expects
he'll persuade Judge Coburn to preside.'

'Will anybody come?' Fearfully she scanned the headlines of the two one-page
extras. Ever mindful that the *Record* was by
far the more popular of the local newspapers.

'They'll come,' Neil insisted. *Will they?* 'Mom and I will be on the phone all day.' He chuckled. 'She'll enlist Eric as well. I promise you, by six p.m. today every man, woman, and child in this town will know about the meeting. And enough will come to spread the word. But no more yakking. Let me rustle up breakfast.'

Neil brought Laurie a breakfast tray of orange juice, scrambled eggs, and coffee, with a second cup of coffee for himself.

'Mom says one of the best post-war inventions is frozen orange juice,' he joshed.

'I can think of a lot of others, too.' She tried for lightness, but her eyes were somber. 'I'm glad you didn't go in to school today.'

'How could I? And I don't mean because of a lack of sleep.' He paused. 'I told the police chief last night that we're engaged.'

'They'll just blame you for bad judgement,' she brushed this aside, fighting tears. *How can that ever be?*

'You are the best thing that ever came into my life,' he said with sudden intensity. 'And I don't mean to let any psycho harm you.'

'Neil, how long can I hide this way?'

'As long as necessary.' His face tightened. 'I spoke to Howie this morning. He'll be over this evening with Karen for some strategy planning.'

Laurie was startled, yet relieved. 'Then

254

they know I'm here?'

'Just Howie and Karen. As your attorney Howie has to know. I dropped by the police station, too.' He sighed. 'They have no clue as to who torched the house.'

'How will we ever track him down?' Laurie gestured in frustration.

'We'll do it,' Neil insisted. 'We'll start to work right now. Let's go back, try to pinpoint anybody – anybody at all – who made nasty remarks in your presence.'

'Most were too cowardly to do that to my face,' she blazed. 'But you know how so many talked behind my back. I felt it wherever I walked. Even in the school lunchroom!' How were they to discover the arsonist who meant to kill her? Was she to spend the rest of her life running away?

Neil leaned forward urgently. 'You never received a threatening phone call? No nasty notes?'

'Nothing.' She spread her hands in a gesture of futility. 'It could have been anybody.'

'The Kendricks are disliked by everybody in town,' Neil conceded, 'but we can't suspect them of burning down the house. They were up in Montreal.'

Laurie debated inwardly for a moment. Her life was at stake. No secrets now. 'The Kendricks battled a lot,' she said. 'The walls in the house are thin. I heard things they wouldn't want me to hear.'

'Like what?' Neil tensed into alertness.

'It seems that he served a prison term.' Laurie searched her mind for small details she'd overhead. 'I gather it was a major robbery. He told his wife – this was when he was still in prison, before they were married – that he would live very well once he was out.'

'He'd stashed away a bundle,' Neil interpreted.

'But it seems his partners got to it first. He found nothing. I gather he inherited the house when his mother died.'

'Did you feel hostility from them?'

Laurie shivered in recall. 'She hated me – I suspect it had to do with the ugly rumors. At one point I was afraid she was going to evict me from the apartment. But she didn't—'

'Because they needed the money,' Neil pinpointed. 'So they wouldn't be likely to burn the house down.' He paused in thought. 'Unless they were after the insurance money—'

'The windows in my bedroom were sealed. Whoever started the fire, lighting it first in the living room – blocking my path to the door – meant to kill me. This wasn't an insurance scam, Neil.'

On her lunch hour Beth returned to the

house. 'I'm driving over to the mall again,' she reported. 'You need clothes, Laurie. Give me sizes so that I choose right.'

'She looks great in your retired slacks and blouse,' Neil joshed. 'But yeah, Mom, pick out some clothes.' Now he frowned. 'If you see anybody from Bentonville, don't shop,' he warned.

Laurie shivered. She didn't even own a hairbrush at this point. *Where do I go from here? Beth said Tim is coming. Will I have to go back to New York with him? Everything's so unreal. I can't visualize tomorrow.*

'Let me get going,' Beth said briskly. 'Oh, tell Howie and Karen to come over early – have dinner with us.'

'I'll call him in a few minutes,' Neil promised. 'I'll be making a lot of calls. Some people may need prodding to come to the meeting.'

'Eric and I will call from the book shop – every chance we get.' She frowned. 'But we shouldn't overlap—'

'I'll take people from "A" through "L",' Neil instructed. Meaning people they suspected would be concerned enough to attend the meeting. 'You and Eric tackle the rest.'

'Laurie, don't stir from this room,' Beth exhorted, her eyes compassionate. 'We can't take chances.'

For Laurie the day dragged. Her mind was

in chaos. Some psycho meant to kill her. Much of this town labeled her a Communist. The School Board had voted to fire her. One question taunted her – over and over again. What chance was there for Neil and her to have a life together?

Between phone calls Neil brought her endless cups of coffee. It was as though she was under house arrest. The guest bedroom was a prison cell. Both she and Neil nervous each time the phone rang, at the sound of a car approaching. No one must know she had survived that inferno.

She fought off the temptation to gaze out a window at what had been her apartment. The firemen had left a little past 6 a.m., Neil had told her. Two men from the police department had been sifting through ashes ever since. Searching for human remains. A grisly task, she thought and shuddered.

'The Kendricks own an empty lot now.' Neil's smile was sardonic. 'What a surprise when they return from Montreal.'

At intervals Neil took a break from making phone calls. Reluctantly he admitted he was encountering some resentment that the meeting was being held.

'We've got some positive reaction,' he tried to bolster Laurie's spirits. 'And several people have agreed to discuss the situation.' He shook his head in frustration. 'And some are adamantly against being part of it. But

I'll ask Jim to talk to Judge Coburn. Maybe they'll listen to him.'

After what Neil labeled their picnic lunch – sandwiches on a tray in the guest bedroom – he and Laurie again went over possible suspects.

'Neil, I just can't believe anybody we've mentioned as being hostile to me would resort to arson,' she admitted.

'Think hard,' he persisted. 'Is there anybody else with whom you had unpleasant words?'

'Just that stupid workman who helped Bud Kendrick with the leak on the roof. He's obnoxious. But no, it couldn't be him,' she rejected. 'Nobody in town could have less interest in the possibility of my being a Communist. He's just a dumb jerk.'

'You mean Chuck Madigan,' Neil pinpointed. 'I saw him working around the house with Kendrick. He dropped out of high school in his third year – I had him in one of my classes. Not a political thought in his mind,' Neil agreed. 'Who in hell started that fire?'

Late in the afternoon – well after school was over for the day – Neil called Doris Lowell. She pretended utter bewilderment at the action the School Board had taken. Despite the lack of public announcement this was common knowledge.

'Neil, I was so shocked when I heard that – just because Laurie had made a stupid remark about Boris Kerensky's concert being canceled – the School Board assumed she was a Communist and voted to throw her off the faculty.'

'The Board understood you were quite upset at Laurie's remarks,' Neil pursued. 'I'd like you to appear at the meeting and repeat what you just said to me.'

'I – I don't know that I can. I mean—' Doris was stammering now. 'Laurie did make that remark about the committee's canceling his concert. I'll have to think about it,' she said hastily. 'Goodbye, Neil.'

A call to Pat was more productive – yet ambiguous.

'Sure, Neil – I'll come to the meeting.' Pat was ebullient. 'But I just don't know how helpful I'll be. But I promise – I'll be there. I'll answer any questions you decide to ask me.'

At shortly past 6 p.m. – when Beth was happily in her chef mode – Karen and Howie arrived.

'How're we doing?' Karen asked, after a few moments with Laurie in the guest bedroom. 'I hear the whole town's buzzing about the meeting tomorrow night.'

'I don't know.' Neil was candid. 'My crystal ball is all fogged over.'

260

Twenty-three

The phone lines in Bentonville were overloaded on Friday morning. Last evening's edition of the *Record* had been scathing in its report of the scheduled town meeting, labeled it an act unsupported by town rules. 'Bad elements in this town are taking over. We must take action to eliminate this.' The front-page article, sprawled over three columns, included acid comments by two members of the School Board. Local residents were vocal in their reactions. Those in favor were a small minority.

In the Andrews house, Cynthia Andrews battled for composure while she discussed the meeting with Gil Taylor.

'You know I admire the *Record* for its approach to most subjects, but why did they announce that we'd voted to discharge that Evans woman? It was bad taste under the circumstances.'

'You going to the meeting?' he challenged and cleared his throat self-consciously. 'I have to be over in Linwood all evening with a client.'

'I'll go,' Cynthia said. 'Only because Judge Coburn made a point of calling me and urging me to attend. We have to defend our actions, Gil. We saw out duty, and we did it. The fact that some idiot burned down her house has nothing to do with it.'

'The Kendricks' house,' Gil pointed out. 'And I think the chief jumped too fast in calling it arson. Of course, the Kendricks are obnoxious people. I wouldn't be surprised if they hired somebody to torch the house. I talked to Len McDougal last night – he said they carried heavy insurance with his company.'

'I don't know what they expect to prove at this stupid meeting.' Cynthia's voice was growing shrill despite her efforts. 'How did Judge Coburn put it last night?' She searched her brain. 'Oh, the town meeting is necessary to prove the integrity of this town. How dare Neil Winston call our firing her an act of witch-hunting!'

Sally Mitchell talked with Denise Spencer with one eye on the clock. She had to be at the beauty salon in forty minutes. Beth Winston hadn't needed much effort to persuade her to be at the town meeting tonight. She had plenty to say – but she might as well look her best. There just might be a fair crowd tonight.

'I tell you this is insane!' Denise grunted

in distaste. 'Where does Jim Peters get the nerve to say – right on the front page of this morning's *Enquirer* – that this town has "made a grievous mistake"? That Evans woman is the one who made a mistake!'

'Donald concocted some excuse not to go, but I think it's my duty to be there. You know, speak up for this town. Why didn't she stay in New York, where she belonged?'

Teachers lingered in small clusters in the entrance area to the Bentonville school. The hum of conversation soared to abnormal heights in those last moments before teachers rushed to their classrooms. Those who had not read the *Record*'s inflammatory reaction to the scheduled town meeting had been informed of its contents by friends or neighbors.

'It's an insult to every resident to call that meeting!' one teacher insisted. 'It's like putting us on trial for doing our civic duty!'

'Maybe we did jump to conclusions,' the male gym teacher defied a small group. 'I mean, we don't *know* that she was a Commie. She was just upset about the concert being canceled without some real proof about that musician. Aren't people supposed to be considered innocent until proven guilty?'

'Oh, it wasn't just what she said about the concert being canceled,' a fellow teacher scoffed. 'I hear she's been making cracks since the first day of school.'

'I'll be damned if I'll show up at that meeting. I've got better things to do with my time. I'd expect such craziness from Jim Peters – but how could Judge Coburn go along with such nonsense?'

'Sure, it's tragic that some arsonist killed her – but it's probably totally unrelated.'

In their Manhattan apartment that Friday morning Iris hunched forward over the breakfast table and listened while Tim deplored his sister's impetuosity at critical moments.

'When will Laurie learn not to jump feet first into controversial situations?' He grunted in exasperation. 'And she's so damn stubborn.' He paused. 'And I love her for fighting for what she believes is right.' His smile was lopsided. His eyes troubled.

'It seems to be a family trait,' Iris joshed, but Tim knew she was as concerned about Laurie's welfare as he.

'Damn it, she almost died in that fire! And the bastard that set it – intent on murder – will try again when he finds out she's alive.'

'Convince her that she has to come back to New York with you,' Iris urged. 'According to the woman who called you, she's been fired from the school. What other job will she be able to land there?'

'It's scary to think about why she was fired,' Tim admitted. 'She's not a celebrity, somebody in an important position. Of course, it shouldn't happen to anybody.' He sighed, drained his coffee cup. 'I'd better hit the road.'

'Just make Laurie understand she has to come back to New York,' Iris reiterated. 'Her life is on the line.'

At the garage Tim collected his car, headed out of the city. He was driving against traffic. He'd make it up to Bentonville in two and a half hours, he thought with satisfaction. But the past kept smacking him in the face. Memories of the months in Spain all those years ago, his disillusionment with the Spanish Civil War.

Yet in truth most Americans who fought in Spain felt it was something they should have done – despite the disillusionment that set in. It was a fight to stop Fascism, what George Orwell called 'the cause of the common people everywhere'. It was frightening that here in the United States someone like Laurie could be persecuted for speaking out for justice.

Annoyed at a slow-down in traffic, Tim realized he was low on gas. He hadn't thought to check when he'd taken the car out of the garage – the only thing on his mind to get Laurie out of that hell hole where she'd almost died. He found a gas station, swung off the highway.

'Fill her up,' he said tersely, then felt a rush of guilt and launched into small talk with the operator about the weather.

With Bentonville at last less than five miles away Tim considered a situation that had nagged at him since that nice woman in Bentonville had called. How long before Iris would come home from the TV station to tell him he rated a report in *Red Channels*? Before going to Spain he'd signed petitions, made some contributions to outfits like the International Rescue Committee. Despite the coolness in the car he felt himself begin to perspire.

He thought about the parade of people who could no longer work in a field where they were highly regarded. And it had shocked Iris and him when *Tide* – a trade magazine – had reported that in questioning major sponsors eighty-eight per cent had said they were convinced sponsors and agencies should consider the ideology of artists and writers when hiring.

He read direction signs just ahead. Here was the turn-off that would take him into town. He searched his mind for directions to the Winston house. Belatedly he recalled the frequent references in Laurie's phone conversation to 'Neil'. Was she emotionally involved with him? Another dead end, after this insanity in Bentonville?

266

He drove down Main Street, made the right turn as directed. Minutes later he pulled up before the Tudor-style house that was the Winston home. He flinched as he glanced about the street and saw the remains of the house where Laurie had lived. Again, he broke out in perspiration as he visualized her horror, her frenzied efforts to escape when she awoke to towering flames and smoke – and sealed windows.

He strode up to the door, was startled to see the drapes across the front of the house all drawn open. But then those inside wanted to create the impression there was no one hiding here. He rang the doorbell. Moments later the door swung open.

'You're Laurie's brother, Tim,' the woman guessed with a welcoming smile. 'Please come in. Laurie's in a back room.'

Over a hastily prepared lunch Laurie sat with Tim and Beth in what had become her limited world. She was overjoyed to see Tim, yet simultaneously she was defensive.

'We can drive back to New York late tonight – after the meeting,' Tim said with determination. 'That psycho who started the fire won't follow you.'

'I can't run away, Tim.' She made a stab at eating the tasty lunch Beth had prepared.

'You can't stay here, Laurie!' he protested.

'You'll stay here with us tonight,' Beth told

Tim – ignoring his talk about returning to New York. She glanced from Laurie to Tim. 'Let's just take one hour at a time.'

'What about the psycho who set the fire?' Tim probed. 'Do the police have any leads?'

'Not yet,' Beth told him and sighed. 'It's not going to be easy to track him down.'

'But we can't relax until he's found,' Tim reminded. 'How do we know what he'll try next?' He swung to Laurie. 'You'll be safe back in New York,' he repeated. 'You can't stay here.'

Twenty-four

Neil and Howie arrived at the school over an hour before the meeting was scheduled to begin. Jim Peters had arranged for the necessary permits. The balcony overlooking the gym floor would hold a hundred people. Folding chairs – available for such occasions – had to be set up on the gym floor to seat another two hundred. A table would be brought in to designate an improvised stage area – where Judge Coburn would preside and where Jim Peters, Neil, and Howie would be seated. The final task was to bring in chairs for the four men and the person to be questioned.

'Don't refer to our "questioning" citizens,' Jim had warned earlier. 'We're to "discuss" the situation.'

At last Neil and Howie had completed the necessary tasks. They exchanged a relieved glance.

'All we need now is for people to show up,' Neil said, his smile tinged with unease. Their team had spent long hours – much effort – to ensure that townspeople would attend, yet both he and Howie were sharply conscious that there was no way of knowing if a handful would appear or if the gym would be packed and the loudspeakers set up outdoors would be needed.

'At least the weather's cooperating,' Howie pointed out with shaky optimism.

Neil took a deep, anxious breath. 'We'll need more than that—'

'So you think we'll have a decent turnout?' Jim Peters' voice came to them as he sauntered down the improvised aisle in the gym.

'We've been working like hell for that,' Howie reminded.

'Not everybody's happy about this meeting,' Jim warned, approaching the two men. 'You two won't win any popularity contests with some folks here in town.'

Neil managed a grin. 'I've been called a few dirty names in the past.' He turned to Howie. 'We both have.'

'The three of us,' Jim expanded this. Apprehension lurked in his eyes for a moment. 'I hope I have a newspaper after tonight.'

Howie cleared his throat. 'I've had a few calls from former clients. Former because they just fired me. I'm the enemy. I dared to be part of calling for a town meeting.'

'We called a meeting because this town is at a crossroads.' Neil's voice deepened with frustration. 'It's way off-course. It's up to us to make people realize that we have to get back to normal. I know – we're just one small town. We can't control the rest of the country – but damn it, we've got to make our town see the light.'

'I had a long talk with Martha Madison and Jason Smith,' Jim reported with satisfaction. 'They'll both be here. They're both willing to testify. Oh, pardon me,' he said with exaggerated politeness. 'They're both willing to share their feelings about the School Board's actions.'

'It's people like Martha and Jason who give me hope,' Neil said gently.

'Look, you two—' Jim hesitated for a moment. 'There's no guarantee we can pull this off. After it's over, we may be quite alone.'

'I can't believe that once people know all the facts, once they consider how they've allowed hysteria to sweep them into horrendous suspicions that – that cost Laurie's life' – Howie exchanged a brief glance with Neil. Jim Peters, his face etched with pain, didn't know that Laurie had escaped that blazing inferno – 'I can't believe they won't be horrified – shocked – by their actions.'

'I know we're gambling,' Neil conceded, 'but if people refuse to face the truth tonight – that we've been on a witch-hunt – then there's no place in this town for me. I don't know where I'll go—' He paused, grimaced in pain. 'But I'll clear out of this town. I couldn't go on living in a town I hated.'

Jim was shaken. 'I've watched you grow up, Neil. I went to school with your mother – sat alongside her in the same classroom where you teach these days. I remember when she started going out with your dad. I danced at their wedding. I never thought I'd live to hear you say that. But if we fail tonight, maybe I'll have to say it right along with you—'

'Karen and I are newcomers.' Howie was somber. 'We thought we'd be spending the rest of our lives here. Now I don't know—'

'Good evening to you, gentlemen.' Judge Coburn's voice came to them from the entrance to the gym. 'I'm a bit early – but that's normal for me.'

'Thanks for coming, Alec.' Jim's smile was warm.

'I don't have to tell you,' Coburn said, walking down the aisle, 'my phone's been ringing off the hook since the *Enquirer* told its readers I'd be presiding tonight.' He glanced from one man to the other. 'Not everybody's in favor of this meeting, you know. Of course, I refused to discuss it with all the callers. I told them to get their butts down here. Whatever is to be said on the subject is to be said right here – out in the open.'

'We appreciate your helping us, Judge Coburn,' Neil said, and Howie nodded in agreement.

'I'll tell you the truth,' Coburn confided. 'I took this on at first because I figured I owe Jim that. But then I started to think – something I haven't done much as far as this business goes. I thought it was just a tempest in a teapot – until word came through about the arsonist. I dropped by the book shop this morning and talked to your mother, Neil.' He smiled at Neil's astonishment. 'I've known your mother ever since I can remember. She's a bright woman. We talked. I remember telling her – right after you came back from your freshman year at college and campaigned so hard for our candidate for Congress. I said, "Beth, that boy should go to law school. We need lawyers with his kind of intensity – and integrity."'

'I remember that campaign.' He'd never admitted – back then or even now – that at some future date he wanted to be active in making this a better town, Neil reminded himself. But his chances in politics might die with tonight's meeting. 'I believed in what we were fighting for. Then and now.'

All at once they were conscious of the sound of voices. Jim glanced at his watch. The meeting wasn't to begin for another eighteen minutes – but people were arriving.

'I've coordinated our lists,' Neil told Judge Coburn and pointed to a clipboard on the table where he was to preside. 'These are the people who've agreed to—' He hesitated. 'Who agreed to take part in the discussion.'

'Sponsored by the *Enquirer*,' Jim drawled.

'God, that Cynthia Andrews,' Judge Coburn clucked. 'After you got through talking to her, Jim, she got me on the phone. Kept me on for almost an hour. You'd think this meeting was called just to torment her. And another thing.' His face tightened. 'Under the circumstances I didn't think it was necessary for the *Record* to come out and say the School Board voted Wednesday night to fire Laurie Evans. Cynthia's so damned convinced they were doing The Right Thing.'

'I hear Martha Madison resigned from the Board.' Jim nodded his head in approval. 'We've got a lot of mending to do.'

More people were pouring into the gym. The hum of voices was reaching a noisy crescendo. People were arguing among themselves, Neil noted. Now the four men most involved in carrying through the meeting began to focus on its format.

'Where's your mother, Neil?' Jim asked curiously.

'Oh, she's down with a bad cold,' Neil lied. Mom couldn't leave Laurie alone in the house. Every light would have to be blacked out if nobody was home. It was better to say

Mom was suffering from a bad cold, running a fever. 'Mad as hell that she can't be here.'

They waited a few minutes longer before calling the meeting to order. Neil hurried outside to check on the loudspeakers. At this rate they'd be needed. There wasn't an empty seat in the gym. Dozens stood at the rear.

Karen stood at the steps with a welcoming smile.

'It's going to be a great turn-out,' Neil said with satisfaction.

'Yeah.' Now she went with Neil to check on the loudspeakers.

'They're working,' she confirmed a few minutes later.

Still, a fear lurked in both Neil's mind and Karen's that people might be coming not repentant, but in protest.

Heading back indoors, Neil exchanged brief, warm greetings with Sophie Kahn and her young son.

'Hi, David,' Neil said. 'You're getting to stay up late tonight.'

'Mama said it was all right. That this is a – a special occasion.' But his eyes wore a poignant sadness. He thought Laurie had died in the fire, Neil realized.

Neil and Karen hurried back into the gym – each taking the planned position. Neil on the improvised stage, Karen to marshal those who were to participate to front row seats, cordoned off for this purpose. Now Jim addressed the audience. He made a point of explaining that the *Enquirer* – as allowed by town regulations – had called this meeting. Then he introduced Judge Coburn.

'Ladies and gentlemen, it's highly unusual in Bentonville for a town meeting to be held,' Judge Coburn began. 'In fact, it's the first time within my memory. But then something most unusual – tragic – has happened. You all know Neil Winston—' He paused while a mumbled acknowledgment swept over the crowd. 'Neil accuses this town of witch-hunting. An un-American act. I hope you all realize the extreme seriousness of this accusation. Bentonville was founded back in 1773. We've always prided ourselves on our loyalty to this country. Every July 4th we reassert our pride in our democracy. But something happened recently that puts this pride in peril.' He gazed about those gathered before him. 'A witch-hunt began to take place in Bentonville. A new teacher in our school system has been the victim. The witch-hunt grew to a fever pitch. Some sick, vicious person among us set fire to Laurie Evans' home, sealed the windows so she couldn't escape. We must ferret out this arsonist. He must stand trial. But first we must face the terrible truth that we – our town – is responsible for this reprehensible deed.' Judge Coburn turned to Neil. He ignored the nervous whispering. 'Neil, I understand you've arranged with several people to come up and discuss this situation.'

'Yes, sir.' Neil rose to his feet.

'I suggest you invite each one of them in turn to join us at this table.' The Judge's tone was casual now. 'And if he feels it necessary, Howard Goldberg – who is here to protect Miss Evans' interests – will question each participant.'

'Thank you, Judge Coburn.' Neil turned to the audience. 'We all know what has been happening in this town since the day the concert committee canceled Boris Kerensky's appearance here. That was the day it started. I'd like Doris Lowell to come on stage to talk about this with us...'

Laurie sat curled up in the club chair Neil had brought into the bedroom for her comfort. She tried – futilely – to focus on the copy of *The Cardinal*, which Beth had brought home from the book shop for her. *How can I read at a time like this?*

Beth came into the guest bedroom with yet another round of coffee. 'I spiked this with a bit of rum,' she confided ingratiatingly. 'Neil teases me – he says I'm becoming a closet drinker.'

277

Laurie's eyes sought out the clock. Even her watch had been lost in the fire, she thought in anguish. But she was grateful for the clothes that Beth had bought for her yesterday. Shoes that fit, though at the moment they sat idle beside the club chair. 'Do you suppose the meeting has started yet?'

'Most likely.' Beth nodded.

'Do you believe people will come?' She knew that Neil's professed reason – to make this town realize how low it had sunk – was honest. But she understood, too, that this was a desperate effort on his part to keep her here in Bentonville. To keep her in his life. 'I mean, enough people to have meaning?'

'With Jim Peters and Alec Coburn beating the drums, I suspect they'll come. Not the whole town, of course,' Beth conceded with a flicker of humor. 'But enough to make a difference.'

'Neil thinks so.' *He has to think so to carry on.* 'I mean, the way he raced around town to get equipment to set up the loudspeaker system. And it's not cold this evening – people can't use that as an excuse not to come.' *Why am I chattering this way?*

'It's a pleasant evening,' Beth agreed. 'Mother nature is on our side.'

'It was so sweet of Tim to come,' Laurie said softly. 'Though I don't know what he can do.' He was there in the school gym right now – prepared if he was called upon to speak. The *Record* had reported on his fighting in Spain – labeling him a Commie along with herself. 'Oh, I wish I could be there. I wish I could hear what was happening!'

Beth seemed wrapped in thought. Then she set aside her coffee cup. Her face exuded determination.

'If the loudspeakers are working, we could hear even a block away. There's no chance of rain, though the moon isn't out. No stars. All right, Laurie. We'll drive over near the school, sit there in the car. Nobody will see us in the darkness.'

Laurie glowed. 'Can we?'

'We can,' Beth said. 'I'll bring the car right up to the door. Nobody will see you get in. We'll park a block away. You'll be safe, Laurie. We'll hear what's being said inside.'

Twenty-five

'This is absurd, Neil!' Doris Lowell protested after several detailed questions about her announcement to Laurie that the Kerensky concert had been canceled – and about Laurie's reaction. 'Everybody in town was talking about the cancellation. We all knew that the Linwood committee had canceled there, too – once they realized the situation.'

'What situation?' Neil probed. His calm approach deceptive.

'That Boris Kerensky is a Communist.' Doris's eyes challenged him to contradict this.

'Did our local committee "know" that?'

'Well, ask the committee.' Color flooded Doris's face. 'They'll tell you.'

'I will,' Neil promised. 'But first let's consider how these "rumors" about Laurie Evans' beliefs circulated. I understand that Cynthia Andrews quoted you at the School Board meeting.'

'I haven't the faintest idea what Cynthia said at the board meeting.' Doris was fighting for composure.

'But you did tell Cynthia Andrews that you believed Laurie Evans is – was – a Communist?'

'I did not! I just mentioned Laurie's odd reaction to the concert's being canceled.'

'You spoke with others about this,' Neil pinpointed. And each time, he thought in a corner of his mind, the accusations were embroidered upon.

'Naturally it was discussed.'

'With whom was it discussed?' Howie pounced.

'I don't remember,' Doris said impatiently. 'But when inflammatory remarks are made, it's natural for people to talk about that.' Her voice strident now.

'Specifically, what remarks?' Howie probed.

Doris grunted in impatience. 'She spoke nastily about the Arts League Committee, when they work so hard to bring culture to this town.' Her tone was scathing. Howie, too, was a newcomer to Bentonville.

'Did anyone else hear the conversation that day between you and Laurie Evans?' Neil picked up. He knew Sally Mitchell's little girl had been in the classroom – Laurie said her mother arrived just as Doris was leaving. Another link? With more embellishments?

'Not that I recall,' Doris told him. 'Oh, I think Sally Mitchell walked into the classroom just as I was leaving.'

'Thank you, Doris,' Neil said and turned to face the audience. 'We'd like to talk with Mrs Mitchell if she's here.' He knew she was here – he'd had a volatile conversation with her. He'd seen her arrive at the last minute, along with her husband.

'I'm here.' Sally Mitchell rose to her feet and walked towards the improvised stage area. Neil remembered his mother making sarcastic remarks about Sally Mitchell's avid pursuit of publicity.

Sally took her seat at the table with an air of amusement.

'Mrs Mitchell, I've heard that you spoke with some heat to several ladies among your acquaintances about remarks Laurie Evans made in the presence of your little girl.' Neil kept his voice casual.

Her face tightened. 'Yes. I was upset that my sweet little eight-year-old was exposed to such talk.'

'What talk?'

She was startled for an instant. 'Doris just told you. No mother wants to hear a teacher defending a Communist right in the presence of her impressionable child. And to speak of our committee the way she did!'

'When you use the word Communist, are you referring to Boris Kerensky?'

'Yes.' Sally turned to the audience for a

moment, as though expecting their confirmation.

'How do you know he's a Communist?' Neil pursued.

'That's no secret.' Her voice was sharp now. 'Everybody in town has heard how the Linwood committee canceled him because of that. Everybody knows he's a Communist.'

'Do they?' Howie joined in now. He pulled a sheet of paper from his jacket pocket. 'I have here a copy of an Associated Press dispatch that was received by the *Enquirer* just two hours ago.' He began to read: '"Boris Kerensky cleared by House Un-American Activities Committee. Musician absolved of any Red affiliations." You hadn't heard about that, I take it?'

'Why, no—' Sally stammered. There was a sudden rumble in the audience.

'So Laurie Evans wasn't defending a Communist. She was defending a fine, democratic principle – something your child should know.'

'Are you implying that I – I–' Flustered, Sally Mitchell groped for words.

'I'm implying nothing.' Howie was forceful. 'I'm saying that Laurie Evans was the injured party in this matter – and that this town is guilty of character assassination. This evening we're judging on facts. Not on idle gossip.'

Sally Mitchell leaped to her feet. 'I don't have to sit here and listen to that sort of thing!' Her face aflame, she strode down the aisle, apparently about to leave the gym. Her husband came forward, pulled her back to the chair she had vacated minutes earlier.

'We'd like to talk with Mrs Andrews, please.' Neil's eyes sought her. She wasn't in the front row, where she was scheduled to be. Damn, she'd promised to be here.

'Yes,' Cynthia Andrews called, walking forward with the air of a queen stooping to associate with lowly subjects. 'I'm here because Judge Coburn asked me to be,' she pinpointed. 'But I hope this won't take long. I have out-of-town dinner guests waiting for me to return.'

'You must not be familiar with the reason for this meeting, Mrs Andrews.' Judge Coburn's smile was ironic. 'I gather I didn't make it clear. This town is accused of witch-hunting. A serious charge.'

'Ridiculous,' Cynthia Andrews scoffed. But she sat in the chair vacated by Sally Mitchell.

'Neil Winston doesn't agree – nor does Jim Peters, whose newspaper is sponsoring this meeting. They both claim that this town has acted in a manner forgetful of everything our country stands for. But they're giving us the benefit of being heard. Now,' Judge Coburn summed up, 'are you willing to testify?'

'I didn't realize court was in session,' she snapped.

'Let us make it clear: in truth, this is a courtroom – and we're all on trial. Every one of us – including myself. Now may we continue?'

'I was a member of the School Board that discharged the Evans woman,' she said coldly. 'I'm not ashamed of that. I went out – at considerable effort on my part and with the help of my co-members – to get the facts in the case.'

'Facts that were as fragile as this pencil.' In barely contained rage, Neil snapped the pencil in two.

'No one could expect you to understand.' Her eyes were contemptuous. 'Everybody knows you were infatuated by the Evans woman.'

Neil aborted an impulse to lash out at her. Again, he contrived to sound calm, analytical. 'The School Board discharged her on the strength of vicious rumors that—'.

'I will not sit here and be talked to this way!' she interrupted. 'You talk about facts. Consider them. This woman read Karl Marx, Lenin, Engels. She soaked herself in every Commie book available. What have you got to say about that?'

'Laurie read Marx, Lenin and Engels because she had been working like the devil on a school paper. A paper on The Good and Evil of Trade Unions. Were you informed of that?'

'We know that her brother – and she often boasted about how close they were – fought with the Loyalists in Spain. But he didn't serve in the American army during World War II,' she shot back.

'May I reply to that, please?' Tim rose to his feet, continued without waiting for permission. 'I'm Timothy Evans, Laurie Evans' brother. Yes, I fought with the Loyalists in Spain, with a number of other Americans fearful of the spread of Fascism in Europe. We weren't fighting for Communism, but against Fascism,' he emphasized. 'And I didn't fight in World War II, because I was rejected. I'd suffered a punctured eardrum in Spain. My sister was never a Communist. It was outrageous that she was fired from her job by the local School Board. I would expect this of a town in Communist Russia – or any country under a dictatorship. I wouldn't expect it in small-town USA.' Abruptly he sat down – to a sprinkling of applause.

'We acted as we thought best for this community.' Cynthia Andrews was instantly defensive. A deer caught in blazing headlights.

'Not everybody on the School Board voted to discharge Laurie Evans.' The firm voice of Martha Madison came from the

286

audience. 'I voted against it. I resigned from the Board because I thought this action was reprehensible.'

'You're speaking out of turn!' Cynthia Andrews shouted. 'As you said, you're no longer a member of the School Board.'

'Please, sir, may I speak?' Sophie Kahn – clutching one small hand of her son – was walking towards the informal stage area.

'Of course you may,' Judge Coburn said gently while Cynthia Andrews stalked away. 'Please sit at the table with us.'

Ill at ease but determined, Sophie sat in the chair just vacated by Cynthia Andrews. 'I come here tonight – and I listen.' Sophie sat at the edge of her chair, held David's hand with one of hers as he stood beside her. 'For many days now people say terrible things about Miss Evans, and then—' Her voice broke. She struggled to continue. 'And then some maniac sets fire to her house. All this makes me so afraid—'

'Go on, Mrs Kahn,' Judge Coburn prodded.

'I came here with my David, after the war – because we were afraid to stay in Germany. We ran to safety here in America – where there is justice for everybody, we think. But if here in America such a thing can happen to Miss Evans, what is there here for my son and me? We were so tired of running – after years of being hidden in

Berlin, by one German family after another – eleven in all. New York was frightening to us – so big! But then it was arranged for David and me to come here. We were so happy. Here, we thought – here it will be different. Nobody can condemn us without a trial. A fair, just trial. In America is freedom. But now I don't know anymore. I'm afraid—'

'Mrs Kahn, will you tell us why you believe Laurie Evans is not a Communist?' Judge Coburn asked.

'I have no – what you call them? – facts. I know only from the heart. When a teacher makes a room full of children love her, when she tells them that America is the greatest democracy in the world and that – but wait—' Sophie Kahn pushed David before her. 'David, you tell them.' But he was hesitant. 'Go on, David, say it like Miss Evans taught you. Like you say it to me.'

David began to speak. No other sound in the gym except for his small, light voice. 'We live in the greatest democracy in the world – and it is our duty as Americans to do everything we can to protect our country and to live by the rules of the Constitution. We have a—' He frowned, groping for words. 'We have a great heritage, and we must never do anything to disgrace it.'

'Does that sound to you like someone who is a Communist?' Sophie Kahn demanded, her voice strong with indignation. 'But you – you fine American citizens – do you give Miss Evans a chance to defend herself? Do you go to her and say, "Can this be true?" No!' Her voice was scathing now. 'You build a web of lies – adding more each time they circulate. You build such hatred for her that someone among you sets fire to her house!' She reached to draw David close to her again. 'I was so proud when we were brought here to this beautiful little town, to become real Americans. My heart was so full. I thought, this is the most wonderful thing that can ever happen to us. But now – now I feel only shame. I feel afraid for my son and myself. Maybe tomorrow someone will say about me, "Sophie Kahn is a Communist." They'll take away my job – drive us out of our house. And where will we go? There would be no place for us anymore – except the river.'

A sea of emotional murmurs filled the gym. A woman sobbed.

'Mrs Kahn, thank you.' Judge Coburn turned to those gathered before him. 'I believe we've all learned an important lesson here tonight,' he began.

In the darkness of the car – while the loudspeaker carried Judge Coburn's eloquent words – Laurie reached for the door.

'I have to go in there,' she said in anguish.

289

'I can't let—'

'I'll drive up to the door,' Beth said. 'We'll go in together.'

'A little boy and his new American mother have shown us our guilt,' Judge Coburn's voice continued over the loudspeaker. 'I look into your faces and see that most of you agree. We won't be electrocuted or hanged or go to the gas chamber for the murder of which we're guilty – as much as though *we* torched the house where she lived, sealed the windows to prevent her escape. But let us pray that the knowledge of our guilt will live with us, and make us more tolerant and more understanding. Let us pray that we can learn to live again in the American way. To live with justice and mercy.'

Breathless and distraught Laurie flung the gym door wide. How could she allow that sweet child David – all the children of her class – believe she had died in that fire?

'Miss Evans!' David's voice was shrill with joy. 'You didn't die in the fire!'

Every head in the gathering turned to the entrance. Voices tumbled over one another, rising to a spontaneous – relieved – crescendo. Neil exchanged a swift, triumphant glance with Howie. Their town was returning to normal.

'What a cheap, theatrical stunt!' Cynthia Andrews cried out, on her feet in rage.

'Would you have preferred that Laurie died in that fire?' Neil demanded.

'But to trick us like this—'

'I insisted on that.' Neil was on his feet. 'To protect Laurie. Her life is in danger. A murderer is on the loose in this town. He's tried to kill her once. He may try again.'

'We don't know that fire was mean to kill her,' Cynthia refuted. 'We—'

'We know! Her only escape – through the two bedroom windows – was sealed tight.' Neil sighed. 'I'm sorry that Laurie chose to come here this way before the killer has been found. We don't know when he'll strike again. He – or she – has a sick mind!'

'I know who did it.' A girl at the rear leaped to her feet. Her voice scared but defiant. Claire Mahoney, Neil recognized – she was a high school drop-out. She'd been in his English class three years ago.

'Who did it?' Judge Coburn asked with calculated calm. 'And how do you know this?'

She seemed to be fighting for courage to continue. Neil noted that the police officer on duty at the meeting moved forward.

'Claire, tell us who set the fire,' Neil urged. 'You don't want to be an accessory to attempted murder, do you?'

'I didn't know until after he set the fire.' Claire was on the edge of panic.

'You're in no trouble,' Judge Coburn

intervened. 'Just tell us, who torched the Kendrick house?'

'It was Chuck Madigan,' Claire blurted out. 'He kept talkin' about how she was a traitor to the country. That she came to this town to spy for the Communists. But that's not why he tried to kill her. He was mad because she didn't want to go out with him. I guess I just wasn't good enough for him anymore. And he didn't tell just me he burned down the house,' she said with fresh defiance. 'He told four or five guys at Johnny's Bar last night! As they – they'll tell you.'

Twenty-six

Laurie stood immobile. Encased in shock. Claire Mahoney's words ricocheted in her mind. *I don't have to stay in hiding any longer. We know who tried to kill me!*

She was conscious of the outcries from those gathered in the gym. Of voices swelling to fever pitch. Were they outraged that a murderer existed in their midst – or distraught by the knowledge that they had provided the motive? Did they realize what they had created?

Judge Coburn banged his gavel for order. The clamor subsided.

'This meeting is concluded,' Judge Coburn announced. 'The police will follow up on this matter. And will the young lady—' He paused to speak with Neil for a moment. 'Will Claire Mahoney please accompany the police officer approaching her to the police station to give a statement?'

Slowly the audience was rising to its feet, preparing – almost reluctantly, Laurie thought – to leave the gym.

Beth pulled Laurie close. 'It's over. The

nightmare is over.'

Laurie contrived a shaky smile – still in shock at this startling conclusion. Her eyes sought Neil. There he was, trying to make his way up the congested aisle. Howie and Jim inched forward behind him. She saw Claire Mahoney and the police officer heading for a side exit. For an instant Claire paused to glance in her direction, lifted a hand in the victory sign.

Laurie spied Eric, also heading for the side exit. He lifted a hand, waved to her, and she waved in return.

'Eric's so happy for you,' Beth said.

Laurie was aware of the compassionate glances of those too shy to come forward, thanked those who paused in the exodus to express their relief at the apprehension of the arsonist. Their eyes were eloquent with apology. Now Tim was at her side, hugged her for a moment.

'You're okay,' he murmured. 'I guess you won't be going back to New York with me.'

Pat and Sharon were headed towards her.

'Let's skip lunch at school on Monday,' Pat effervesced, and Sharon nodded in agreement. 'Why don't the four of us–' Her gaze included Karen, who'd made her way to Laurie's side. 'Why don't we have lunch at The Oasis? On me.'

'Great,' Laurie accepted.

A woman and a man – unknown to Laurie

– were making their way towards her. 'That's Martha Madison and her husband,' Karen told Laurie.

'It was awful – what this town put you through,' Martha said. 'But we're back on course. And we're lucky to have you in our school.'

'Thank you.' Laurie's face was luminous. People understood.

David Kahn, followed by his mother, shoved his way to Laurie. 'You'll be in class on Monday?' His eyes clung to hers – pleading for reassurance.

Laurie bent to kiss him. 'I'll be there, David.' She reached a hand to Sophie. 'Thank you. You both were wonderful. This town should be very proud of you.'

There would be much grief in the country before the nightmare witch-hunting – assaulting the nation like a plague – was at last put to rest, Laurie thought – but here in Bentonville it was over. There would be those in this town – Cynthia Andrews and Gil Taylor among them – who would harbor the same thoughts spouted by the likes of Senator Joe McCarthy. But they'd lost their clout here. Reason had returned to Bentonville.

Laurie's face lighted. Neil was at last approaching, along with Howie and Jim.

'Why don't we all go over to our house?' Howie invited in high spirits – dropping an arm about Karen. 'There's a bottle of champagne chilling in the fridge – just waiting for a major occasion.' He grinned. 'Okay, so I planted it there before the meeting.'

When the last morsel of one of Beth's inspired lunches had been consumed, the coffee pot drained, Laurie and Neil walked with Tim to his car.

'Drive carefully,' Laurie told him. 'It was great of you to come.' She sent him a gamine grin. 'But I expected it.'

'I wouldn't have missed it.' Tim glowed. 'I might even be able to do an article about it for the magazine.' He considered this for a moment, sighed philosophically. 'The powers-that-be may argue that it's too controversial,' he admitted. 'I'm proud of you, Laurie. You fought for what you believe in.' He focused on Neil now. 'Take care of her, will you? You never know what she'll come up with next.'

'Reserve the Thanksgiving weekend,' Neil said with an air of sudden inspiration and turned to Laurie. Their eyes in unspoken communication. *He's talking about a Thanksgiving wedding.* Oh, yes! 'Your presence may be required.'

'Iris and I will stand by,' Tim promised, his smile brilliant. He reached to kiss Laurie goodbye. 'Thank God that creepy arsonist is behind bars. He'll stay there a long time.

But, Laurie,' he pleaded with mock ferocity, 'please, try to stay out of trouble.'

Hand in hand, Laurie and Neil walked back into the house. Beth was on the phone. She gestured for silence while she listened.

'I'm going out to the kitchen for bread,' Neil whispered. 'Let's drive out to the lake and feed the ducks.'

'Yes.' Laurie understood. This was Neil's way of saying, 'All's right with the world again.'

Wrapped in euphoria, she waited for Neil to return, for Beth to be off the phone. Neil's remark about the Thanksgiving weekend was etched on her brain. What she'd feared could never happen might just happen on Thanksgiving weekend. *I'm not misinterpreting Neil, am I?*

Beth put down the phone, took a deep breath. 'That was Eric.'

'It was sweet of him to let you take off this morning,' Laurie said. Saturday was the shop's busiest day.

'I'm going in now. But first—' She paused as Neil came back into the room. 'Nobody else knows yet, but Eric is selling the shop to me and moving to New York. We talked about it early this morning.'

'Oh, good for him!' Laurie was enthusiastic.

'He said you gave him the courage to do

what he'd yearned to do for twenty years,' Beth told Laurie. 'I'm buying the shop.' Her face lit mischievously. 'And his house. He'll stay here in town until all the legal papers are handled, but then he's off for his personal paradise. You know,' she said whimsically, 'theater, ballet, opera, all those fantastic museums. He's making it very easy for me financially.'

'But why the house?' Neil was bewildered.

'Oh, this house is too big for me. All the unnecessary work entailed.' She clucked in suspect distaste. 'Eric's house is small – but plenty large for me. This will be yours.' Beth's gaze moved from Neil to Laurie. 'It's a house that demands a family.'

'Mom!' Neil moved forward to hug her. Laurie felt tears fill her eyes. She, too, crossed to Beth and embraced her.

'Of course, this is all a bit premature,' Laurie pointed out.

'Give us a little time,' Neil scolded. 'We're going over to the lake to feed the ducks, Mom. Shall we drop you off?'

'That short trip to the shop?' Beth scoffed. 'I'll walk. Good for the soul.'

Laurie and Neil were silent on the drive out to the lake. They sat close together – her head on his shoulders. Her perfect small town had redeemed itself. She felt she belonged now – was accepted.

'I don't suppose we'll be going out to

Montauk over the Thanksgiving weekend,' Laurie said at last, with simulated regret.

'Oh, absolutely,' he corrected. 'Providing you agree to a Thanksgiving Day wedding. We'll honeymoon at Gurney's – the way I'd planned all along.'

'I thought you'd never ask.'

Wrapped in euphoria, they left the car to feed the eager ducks.

It was as though she had been in the grip of a terrible illness, Laurie mused – and now the crisis had passed. She was well again – and the world was beautiful. Life more precious than before the awful siege.

She suspected that the battle just fought in Bentonville would be repeated in villages and towns and cities throughout the nation – but freedom would survive.